PEACOCKS KILL

Janet Moller

authorHOUSE®

AuthorHouse™ UK
1663 Liberty Drive
Bloomington, IN 47403 USA
www.authorhouse.co.uk
Phone: 0800.197.4150

Published by AuthorHouse 04/11/2016

ISBN: 978-1-5246-3200-7 (sc)
ISBN: 978-1-5246-3201-4 (hc)
ISBN: 978-1-5246-3199-4 (e)

Print information available on the last page.

THE CLOCK STRUCK EIGHT.

Matilda heard the muffled gunshot but wasn't particularly concerned. She lived in a small English village buried deep in the countryside surrounded by farms, and every farmer had a gun. Pot shots at rabbits were a common occurrence.

She continued picking succulent black berries for a pie she planned to bake, strolling slowly to the end of the lane, enjoying the mid-summer sun dancing on her face, the chorus of bird song a delight to the ears, the fragrance of flowers in full bloom wafting through the breeze, heady and intoxicating. Bliss!

There's nothing like the peace and tranquillity of England's green and pleasant land, apart from the odd gunshot or two, she thought, and hitching the basket of fruit into the crux of her arm, opened the wooden gate to her two up, two down hundred-year-old stone and thatched roof cottage. Carefully picking her way along the uneven garden path, she stopped now and again to inspect the fruits of her green fingers.

My, those strawberries are just about ripe for picking. Mmmm, fresh clotted cream and strawberries. Now that's something to look forward to.

Opening the unlocked back door, she walked along the narrow flag stone passage to the kitchen, where she deposited the berries in a bowl by the sink, ready to wash, after having a cup of her favourite Earl Grey and a couple of digestive biscuits.

Glancing at the kitchen clock on the way to the lounge, she noticed it was nearly midday.

Matilda opened the lounge door, put the tray on a small wooden coffee table near her favourite winged armchair, and assured me afterwards, she didn't notice anything untoward until after she'd poured herself a cuppa. Sitting back in the chair with the plate of biscuits on her lap, she happened to glance at the antique grandfather clock standing in the far corner of the room.

The clock face showed eight am.

That's odd, thought Matilda. *I wound this clock only yesterday.*

After putting the plate of biscuits back onto the tray, she walked over to rewind the clock.

To do this, she had to pass by the settee; and that's when she saw the body, mostly hidden behind the piece of furniture; a man lying on his stomach, head turned to one side exposing the bullet hole.

The man was young, Matilda guessed in his early thirties, blond hair matted with congealing blood slowly oozing into a sticky puddle onto her cream coloured carpet. The contrast in colours was shocking. He wore a dark grey suit, light blue shirt and navy tie and was clutching a silk scarf in his right hand that was partially hidden by the way he had fallen on his arm.

Now, to understand why Matilda did what she did next, involves a little bit of explaining.

She is most definitely not your typical elderly gentlewoman living a quiet, peaceful village existence. Before her retirement two years ago, she had run a successful private detective agency, which was still in business, specialising in stolen art treasures, and her reputation for discreetness and swift results had made her very popular with art collectors' world- wide who shunned publicity for various reasons.

So, her experiences in the murky world of dubious art dealing, sometimes requiring involvement with the criminal element, combined with all the travelling she'd done over the years, often on her own, meant Matilda was not easily scared.

To top it off, she was also an enthusiastic amateur archaeologist who could rough it with the best of them.

So, the first thing she did was remove the scarf from the corpse's hand. It belonged to her, and she thought it very odd it was in his possession.

After tucking the scarf in her cardi pocket, and glancing around the scene of the crime, she phoned the police and spoke to the one and only constable stationed in the small village, told him she had found the body of a young man in her lounge who'd been shot in the head, and please would he come and do his job.

After a stunned silence, Police Constable Harvey told Matilda he was on his way and not to disturb anything.

Whilst waiting for P.C.Harvey, she decided, naturally, to have a look around the rest of the cottage. After all, the murderer could still be lurking somewhere. The murder was recent, as blood still oozing from the head wound and the body warm to the touch could vouchsafe.

Armed with her licensed shotgun, which she'd removed from her gun safe under the stairs, Matilda checked the other rooms and the front garden and found nothing amiss.

So, after locking the front and back door as a precaution in case the murderer did decide to return to the scene of the crime, she went back to the lounge and stared at the body, wondering who the young man was, and why he'd met his demise at the back of her settee, and why on earth was he clutching her silk scarf which she always kept in her bedroom.

It was a gruesome murder, all the more shocking for it to have happened in her lovely cottage in a supposedly crime free village.

A clattering noise shattered the silence.

It took Matilda a few seconds to realise it was her fax machine.

She locked her gun away and hurried upstairs to the office she'd organised in one corner of her bedroom, and picked up the fax. The printout only showed a lot of letters and numbers all jumbled randomly, making no sense at all.

On hearing P.C. Harvey's heavy footsteps hurrying along the garden path, she put the fax on the office table, and went down stairs to the front door to let him in.

'Good afternoon, Constable Harvey. Come through to the lounge. The body's lying behind the settee.'

'Right, Mrs Syndham. Have you touched anything at all since you phoned me?'

'Not since I phoned you, no,' answered Matilda, and led the way to the lounge.

P.C. Harvey stood surveying the scene for a few minutes, fingering his chin thoughtfully.

'Do you recognize the victim Mrs. Syndham? Have you noticed him around these parts at all?'

'No, I'm afraid not. We don't get many strangers here as you know. It's so odd. Why would a young man like that get murdered in my lounge in this out of the way village? It just doesn't make any sense!'

Police Constable Harvey was a well- respected policeman in these parts, very thorough in his job, and quite able to apprehend the odd chicken thief, to lock up a drunken driver and generally keep law and order. This type of crime, however, was not your typical village affair, so he decided a call to the C.I.D. offices in the nearby city of Rourke was in order.

And then I arrived, expecting a peaceful couple of weeks recuperating from the ravages of city life, being fussed over by my favourite aunt.

Instead, I found a policeman in the hallway on the telephone, and aunt tut tutting over a corpse.

'Oh Ella! What a lovely surprise to have you arrive early. Really my dear, you couldn't have timed it better with all that's been happening.'

That's my Aunt Matilda.

Enter the Bill.

I'll confess I can be as nosey as the next person, so, with P.C. Harvey still on the phone, and undeniably feeling a sense of trepidation, I left my suitcase at the bottom of the stairs and followed aunt to the lounge, carefully making my way over to the settee to look at the body, and then immediately wanting to throw up.

Matilda took one look at my face, grabbed my arm, and frogmarched me into the kitchen where she pushed me onto a chair, pressed my head between my knees and told me to take deep breaths, which I duly did.

After a few minutes the nausea sensation began to ease and I struggled to sit up straight. Aunt Matilda had had her hand firmly pressed on the nape of my neck, keeping my head exactly where she wanted it.

'I thought you were made of stronger stuff, Ella.'

I looked at her blankly.

She handed me a glass of water and after gulping down a few mouthfuls, I felt the colour coming back into my face and the horrible queasiness receding.

P.C. Harvey walked into the kitchen and sat at the table next to me.

'Are you alright?' he asked, sounding quite concerned.

Matilda stood staring at me for a minute before speaking.

'It wasn't just the sight of blood making you feel like that was it Ella?'

'No aunt.' I took a deep breath. 'The thing is, I know or rather knew your corpse.'

P.C. Harvey pulled out his notebook, licked the end of his pencil, turned to a clean page and looked at me expectantly.

'Well,' I said, trying to collect my thoughts, 'his name is or rather, was Philip Westbury. In fact I hardly knew him, as we'd only met about a week ago. It was at the library. I was researching old silver, looking up the different hallmarks so I'd have some idea of the age of items at a local antique auction I wanted to visit. There was a book I needed that was high up on one of the shelves. As I tried to reach it, this man leant over my shoulder and kindly got it for me. When he glanced at the title he mentioned different pieces of silver he'd collected over the years. We got chatting and ended up having coffee in the library coffee shop.'

'Did he tell you anything about himself?' asked P.C. Harvey.

'Only that his name was Philip Westbury. He said he hadn't been in town long, and how nice it was to meet someone as interested in old silver as he was.'

'Did you tell him much about yourself?'

I thought about that before answering. Thinking back, I could see I'd definitely told Philip more about myself than I had learnt about him.

'I did tell him a bit,' I hedged.

'Did you mention your aunt and this cottage?'

'I could have done. I can't really remember. It was a casual acquaintance. I never saw him again.'

Then the doorbell rang and in walked the various personages from Rourkes' C.I.D.

It was obvious who was in charge.

A tall well-built man with short brown hair, topping a bullet shaped head announced he was Inspector Stuart, and took immediate control, dispatching his underlings to go about their various jobs of investigating a murder.

After inspecting the body, he allowed P.C. Harvey to do the introductions and then proceeded to grill Aunt Matilda and I as to what we knew; making notes on anything he thought was relevant.

It took the police a good few hours to complete everything they needed to do initially, checking for fingerprints, recording aunt's and my statements on a dictaphone, taking photographs, and then the police surgeon arriving and examining the body before arranging transport for a post mortem, not that there could be any mistaking how Philip met his demise.

Finally they left Blackberry Cottage after sealing the lounge door and the inspector cautioning aunt not to leave her front and back doors unlocked again. There wasn't much she could say in defence to that statement!

We obviously were not allowed to stay at the cottage until all police work was completed, so decamped to the Bubbling Brook pub situated not far from the cottage along the banks of the river.

Inspector Stuart informed us he would be back in the morning to go over our statements in case we remembered anything else and then would have them typed up prior to us signing them.

THE FAX.

It was eight -thirty in the evening, and twilight had begun to settle. The sun was just visible peeping above the rolling hills, golden rays making a stunning backdrop of country scenery that usually never failed to move me each time I visited the cottage.

This time, however, I was in no mood to be moved.

We'd eaten a sparse supper of cold meats and salads, as neither of us felt particularly hungry, and carried our coffee to the pub's conservatory facing the narrow river. From where we were sitting, we could see the outline of the cottage in the distance.

I still couldn't believe what had happened.

Philip had seemed such a nice person. Nevertheless, somebody hated him enough to murder him. But what could possibly be the motive behind the killing?

Questions were milling round and round in my mind. For starters, why was he here today?

According to Inspector Stuart, the gunshot Matilda heard whilst blackberry picking, was probably the one that had killed him.

Had I told him I was coming for a visit?

I might have done. I honestly couldn't remember.

Was the interest in silver just an excuse to strike up a conversation with me?

My initial liking for Philip was changing rapidly. Even though he was dead, I was very angry at the thought he had put my beloved aunt in jeopardy.

'The fax! I forgot about the fax.'

Aunt Matilda shot up from her chair, raced across the conservatory and disappeared.

'What fax?' but aunt didn't answer.

After a couple of minutes she returned, carrying her carpetbag.

'With all that's been going on, I totally forgot about this strange fax I received just after I found that young man's body. I popped it in my bag when I knew we'd be coming to the pub. Look, Ella, what do you make of that?' handing me an A4 sheet of paper.

I looked at it for a minute. It was baffling, to say the least.

'It makes no sense at all, aunt. Just a load of letters and numbers jumbled together. How strange… You say it came just after you found Philip?'

'Yes. Why? You don't think it could have anything to do with the murder do you?'

'I don't know, but it's possible, especially as you've never received a fax like that before, and just think of the timing. Don't you think it's a bit coincidental?'

'Maybe so.'

We stared at the piece of paper, trying to figure out what it meant.

'Have you any idea who sent it?'

'No, I haven't a clue. I don't recognise those numbers at the top of the page, and there's no cover letter to say who sent it. It's an absolute puzzle.'

As Matilda said that, she bounced up from her chair again.

'Maybe that's it. Maybe it is a puzzle or a code or something. I know this will probably sound ludicrous, but could this garbled message be so important that Philip risked hanging around waiting for it before he was shot? The murderer followed him to the cottage, killed him, and then heard me come through the back door. So, whoever it was ran out the front door and missed getting it.'

Matilda stopped speaking.

The same thought struck her as it did me.

Were we in possession of a document that was so important it was worth murdering for?

'No!' She answered my unspoken question. 'I refuse to believe that. I really think I'm talking nonsense. But, anyway, I'll phone Inspector Stuart now and tell him about it.'

When Matilda came back to the conservatory, she said the inspector was sending P.C. Harvey around to the cottage to pick it up.

'But what I have done Ella, is used the pub's photocopier to copy it. I wouldn't mind trying to find out where it came from. You don't mind do you?'

What else could I say but, 'No aunt, I don't mind, not really. I'm pretty sure it doesn't have anything to do with Philip's murder, so, where's the harm.'

'Now this is also really odd,' and Matilda pulled a silk scarf out of her cardigan pocket.

'That young man was clutching this scarf. I always keep it in my bedroom, so why he had it goodness only knows.'

'That is weird. Any ideas at all?'

'No, my dear, not a clue. I received the scarf as a thank you for research work I did for a clothing company. It made a bit of a change from dealing with criminals. They wanted authentic Ethiopian patterns of the Queen of Sheba era for a range of clothing accessories they were producing. One of the designers knew a friend who knew my interest in this period of history. I was contacted and asked if I would be willing to give some input, which, of course, I did. Apart from my usual fee, I was given this scarf as a present because one of the designs I helped with apparently is reproduced in the scarf. I can't see it myself, but, heigh ho.'

'How long ago was this, aunt?'

'Oh, let me see, about a year ago. Not much more than that, I'm sure. Swingen Linen, that's the name of the company, wanted to have the line ready for their summer collection, which came out two months ago in June. We are now in August, so yes, a year ago last June.'

I held the scarf up to the light.

Frankly, I didn't think much of it, as the pattern, if you could call it that appeared distorted and the colours were bland, mainly different shades of brown and green with black lines meandering through them.

I shrugged, and gave the scarf back to aunt. She popped it in her carpet bag alongside the fax.

'I can't even begin to think what Philip was doing with it.'

'Same here. Anyway, I don't know about you but I'm tired. Let's go to bed. We'll discuss this tomorrow.

Decision made.

We passed an uneventful night.

To say I slept well would be an exaggeration, but I felt more like myself when aunt woke me with a cup of tea.

'Morning Ella. It's a gorgeous day. I almost thought I'd dreamt the happenings of yesterday until I opened my eyes and looked at my surroundings. I wonder when we'll be able to go back to the cottage. Were you able to get some sleep?

I yawned whilst pulling myself into a sitting position and leant against the pillows.

'Thank you for the cuppa, and yes, I nodded off eventually. What time is it?'

'Just after eight. I'm not sure what time Inspector Stuart will come around, but I'd rather be up and about. I can't say I warmed to him very much though. Bit too officious.'

Aunt plopped herself down on the dressing table stool.

'I checked that fax, Ella. I think it was too much of a coincidence it coming through at that time. I'm sure I'll be able to trace where it was sent from.'

Alarm bells immediately clanged in my head and just about everywhere else. I looked at aunt with misgiving. When she gets the proverbial bee in her bonnet, there's no stopping her. During the course of my growing up, I'd been involved in various adventures due to her insatiable curiosity, but murder! I wasn't sure I was keen to play along with her on this one.

But aunt was on a roll.

'The more I think about that young man murdered in my cottage, the angrier I get. What a waste of a life and, frankly, I feel my cottage has been defiled if that's not too strong a word.'

There was a knock on the door. It was Bob, the pub's proprietor, informing us of Inspector Stuart's arrival.

Ten minutes later I went downstairs to the conservatory, where aunt and the inspector were discussing the previous day's happenings.

'Good morning Miss Stanbridge.'

'Good morning Inspector Stuart.'

Were you able to remember anything else that could help?'

'No, Inspector. I'm sorry.'

'Well, you know how to get hold of me if you do. I've given your aunt my telephone number. Please use it regardless how trivial you may think something is. P.C.Harvey gave me the fax. I've my doubts as to whether it has any bearing on the case, but I'll have it checked out.'

'Have you found the gun yet?' I asked.

'No. It's possible the murderer threw it in the river or just took it with him. I've police combing the whole area, plus a couple of divers checking just in case. If it's around we'll find it. Here is your statement. Read it and if you agree with what's been typed, just write your signature on each page.'

I read through the statement. It looked ok so I signed it. Aunt did the same to hers.

Inspector Stuart stood to go. He was apologetic about having to keep the cottage sealed for a few more days, but was sure things would return to normal very soon.

Aunt Matilda came back to the conservatory after seeing the inspector off the premises.

She wanted to track down the fax number.

'There's no time to lose, Ella. I've a funny feeling about this whole affair, and regardless what Inspector Stuart thinks, that fax is important.'

She looked at her watch.

'Sylvia will be in the office.'

'No she won't. It's Sunday.'

Matilda smiled at me.

'I know Sylvia will be at the office because she told me so the other day. She needs to catch up on paperwork apparently. I'll phone her with the numbers. She'll trace it for me.'

Sylvia had been aunt's secretary and was now a PI in her own right, continuing the work aunt used to do, along with a dozen others. PIArt.Inc. had offices in London, Paris, Milan and New York.

Sylvia rang back within fifteen minutes with a name, address and telephone number.

'The fax number belongs to an art dealer called Frederick Short. He has an art shop in Chelsea.'

It was as simple as that.

Aunt Matilda was puzzled.

'I've never heard of this man, Ella. Why on earth is he sending me faxes?'

'Do you want to phone and find out? Or better still, let's give the information to Inspector Stuart and he can find out.'

Matilda snorted in exasperation.

The upshot was not only did she persuade me to phone, but when there was no reply, she convinced me the only thing we could possibly do for Philip Westbury was to get in the car and drive to London to check out Mr. Frederick Short ourselves.

'You do realize today is Sunday. What chance is there of finding Mr. Short in his shop?'

'Well, these places are often open on Sundays and just think, there won't be much traffic on the roads and anyway, I can't imagine sitting here all day twiddling my thumbs. Let's just go.'

And that's what we did.

SHORT'S ART GALLERY.

The journey to London was actually rather pleasant as the day was sunny, sporting azure blue skies, cotton wool clouds and picture card scenery; the total antithesis to violent murder.

We arrived in London early afternoon, and with the help of the sat nav, located Short's Art Gallery. It was situated on the corner of a seedy looking street named Colebank, and I found it hard to imagine any art gallery thriving in such an area,

We pulled up outside the entrance.

The gallery had two bay windows with a mediocre, fading water-colour displayed on a miniature easel in each one. The windows obviously hadn't seen any soapy water for ages, and the woodwork surrounding them needed a good sanding and repaint. The front door was made of smoky glass shaped in an oval, surrounded by dark ebony wood. What really startled me was the large hairy spider engraved on the glass.

'Ugh! Aunt, remember that tarantula I found in that box of bananas a friend sent me? We caught the thing in a wastepaper basket and threw it out of the window hoping it would die of cold because it was winter.'

'Yes, I remember. I always felt we should've given it to a zoo or something. Terrible to feel guilty over a spider.'

I pulled the bell chain that was hanging on the right hand side of the door. I could hear it ringing faintly in a distant part of the gallery.

We waited for Mr. Short to appear.

He never did.

'It's Sunday. He didn't answer the phone. He's probably spending a pleasant afternoon with his family.'

Aunt Matilda stepped forward and tried the wooden knob of the door handle. The door swung open.

It was dark inside, mainly due to the dirty state of the bay windows, but also our eyes had to get accustomed to the gloom after being used to the bright sunshine outside.

'Mr Short! Are you here?' I shouted.

'Do you have to yell like that,' complained Aunt Matilda. 'You'll wake the dead.'

We walked down a couple of steps into the gallery. There were various paintings, etchings and statues on display, looking as though they'd been there for years.

Turnover in this business was not good.

'He should get someone to come in and clean now and again. This statue is covered in dust. I can't make out any details at all.'

'I should hope not. The dust is the only thing giving it a bit of modesty.'

Matilda could be prudish at times.

'Hullo! Anyone at home?'

To tell you the truth, this place was beginning to give me the creeps.

'Let's go to the back of the shop, Ella. Maybe he's hiding there.'

Matilda strode across the gallery floor towards a dark red velvet curtain which appeared to be concealing an entrance.

She pulled back the curtain with a flourish, stepped into a room and stopped dead in her tracks.

I peered over her shoulder, and saw two feet sticking out from behind a desk.

'Mr Short I presume.'

I wonder why I wasn't surprised.

THE PUZZLE OF THE SCARVES.

We walked into what was obviously an office.

Filing cabinets lined two adjacent walls, a desk and overturned office chair was on the left as you walked into the office. On the right was a photocopier and fax machine.

Aunt Matilda leant over the body.

He had a bullet wound through the left temple and had obviously been sitting in the office chair before being shot. The momentum of falling had overturned the chair. There was blood oozing out of the wound.

'I think the killer of Philip and what appears to be Mr. Short are the same person'

'For goodness sake aunt, that's really jumping to conclusions!' although to be honest I was thinking the same.

'No, I don't think so. The MO is the same and you might think I'm being fanciful, but I just know the fax is the connection. I'm sure of it.'

I looked at the corpse.

Mr. Short had not been so short when he was alive. He was approximately six feet tall, thin, in his fifties I would have thought, with greying brown hair framing a nifty goatee beard, just the type of look one would associate in an owner of an art gallery.

I shuddered.

'What on earth is going on, aunt? If the killer finds out we've been here I'd hate to think how we're going to end up. Maybe just like that.'

JANET MOLLER

And I pointed theatrically to the unfortunate Mr. Short.

'Oh nonsense! Let's see what we can find.'

Aunt Matilda's customary rosy cheeks were beginning to glow again after the initial shock of finding Mr. Short dead. On her face was a look I'd seen before, the look of the hunter tracking its quarry, although the quarry was usually an art thief trying to off load a valuable painting or antique.

On the desk was a computer. It was switched on, the screen showing a psychedelic screen saver. Aunt put on a pair of thin rubber gloves she always kept in her carpetbag, jiggled the mouse and looked at the file name that came up on the screen. It read MAKOKOSHLA.

'What a peculiar word. It looks like a strange language, maybe African, which is all very interesting but I am now phoning the police.'

Matilda stared at the word.

'Hold on two tics. You know, Ella, I think that's a good guess on your part. I've seen that word before, but for the life of me I can't think where. Never mind. It will come back to me. I'm going to zap on it and see what happens.'

Matilda clicked the mouse and immediately the screen was filled with a jumble of letters and numbers similar to the fax sent to the cottage. I went to the printer, which was switched on and aunt clicked to print a copy. There was nothing else in the Makokoshla file, and we left the computer as we'd found it.

Matilda walked towards a door at the back of the office. She opened the door and looked up and down the lane.

'Do you think the murderer heard us coming into the shop and ran out of this door? It leads into an alley. Easy for the murderer to get away unnoticed.'

'Wouldn't we have heard the shot?'

'Not if he used a silencer.' She closed the door. 'We'll have a quick look round before we phone the police.'

The fax machine yielded nothing; neither did the telephone pad or notebook which was on the desk. There were just notations for the benefit of Mr. Short's memory.

18

However, in his address book, the name Swingen Linen was written and underlined heavily with yesterday's date printed by the side of it so Matilda jotted down the address and telephone number. Why would Mr Short be interested in Swingen Linen?

And then the strangest discovery of all.

Hidden in plain sight, another silk scarf, looking amazingly similar to the one given to Matilda by Swingen Linen; only this one was on show as a piece of artwork, framed and hanging on the wall behind one of the red curtains. When the curtain was pulled back, it hid the frame from view.

Without being asked, I put on the gloves, lifted the frame down and removed the backing. Matilda popped the scarf into her carpet bag and I rested the frame against a stack of others leaning against a wall.

Yes, you are quite correct. I did feel like an accomplice assisting my aunt in nefarious doings.

Anyway, I then phoned the police and within minutes the whole shebang arrived.

Our story was we just happened to visit the gallery as sometimes in these out of the way places little gems could be found. We found the body whilst looking for the proprietor.

'And that's all we can tell you, constable,' said Matilda to one of the policeman taking notes.

After sealing off the shop, whilst the crime team got on with their job, we were taken to the local police station and once again made statements which we duly signed. They seemed satisfied for now with our explanations, and then, after a four hour wait, presumably whilst our credentials were checked, we were allowed to leave. I was surprised no mention was made of the happenings in aunt's cottage. Maybe we were on a different data base. Neither of us had volunteered that information because it seemed so incriminating. That was a mistake.

It was getting late by the time we pulled up outside the Bubbling Brook.

I glimpsed the shadow of a police car up the lane stationed outside the cottage. I presumed Inspector Stuart had decided on this precaution.

I parked the car whilst aunt made a pot of tea from the tea making paraphernalia supplied in our rooms. We settled ourselves in the conservatory, drinking and eating digestive biscuits whilst we examined the printout more closely.

'You know aunt; I can't help wondering where this is going to lead. We've got two dead bodies, a fax and printout of jumbled letters and numbers, two weird looking scarves and no idea what Philip was doing in your cottage in the first place?'

'I know Ella. It really is a mystery. I must try and remember where I've heard the name Makokoshla before. That's really puzzling me, and we need to find out the connection between Philip and Frederick Short, if that was Frederick Short we found. Philip was interested in old silver and Mr. Short dealt in antiques of sorts; maybe Philip had an arrangement with the art dealer in whatever he found. Maybe there's a family connection somewhere, an uncle or grandson. Maybe they were business partners.'

Aunt Matilda stopped talking, a frown creasing her forehead.

I kept quiet.

She eventually began speaking again.

'Do you think my PI business is linked in any way? As you know my speciality was finding lost and stolen artwork. I think I'll phone Sylvia in the morning and ask her to run names through our database. Who knows what might pop up?'

'Well, that's an idea I guess, although my idea of a couple of weeks R&R seems to be fading away rapidly,' I said, grinning at aunt.

Guilt swept across Matilda's face.

'I'm so sorry Ella. With everything that's been happening I haven't even thought to ask how your work is progressing and how is Dave or is it Will, I can't remember.' Her voice tailed off.

I gave her a quick hug.

'Don't look so guilty, aunt. I'm only joking. It isn't every day we almost witness two murders occurring in quick succession. My tale of forsaken love pales totally into insignificance compared to that. Oh, and it was Will actually. But,' I paused dramatically, 'work is going great. My lectures on The Queen of Sheba: Myth or Legend were well received and Prof Philips was quite happy in my taking at least six weeks off before the next dig season starts. Will, you'll be pleased to hear, is history. You were spot on when you said I'd be bored within a month. Actually, the second date did it for me. I just couldn't muster any enthusiasm in standing still in a bird hide for hours on end again waiting for a spotted whatever to materialise. Anyway, Will said I was too fidgety to ever be a good bird watcher so we parted company quite amicably.'

I glanced at my watch. Nearly midnight.

'Come aunt, off to bed. We'll continue discussions on plan of action in the morning.'

CHIEF SUSPECTS.

Monday dawned with Inspector Stuart storming into the pub demanding to know what we'd been doing at Frederick Short's art gallery yesterday afternoon!

The Chelsea Police had kindly let the inspector know an elderly lady (aunt was not amused at the elderly connotation) and her niece residing in his jurisdiction had unfortunately stumbled upon a murder, only to be told this was the second one in two days.

I could see we topped the list of chief suspects.

Inspector Stuart was not in the best of moods. Fair cop, I thought, knowing we didn't have a snowballs chance in hell of palming him off with a concocted story.

'I asked a colleague to trace the fax, Inspector,' said Matilda. 'I was very curious about it, and as you didn't think it had any involvement with the case I couldn't see any harm. So, as we'd nothing better to do on Sunday, we decided to visit Mr. Short, never dreaming we'd find him dead.'

Inspector Stuart stopped pacing the room and turned to look at aunt, eyes glaring at her from his bullet shaped head. Not a pretty sight.

'Your meddling ends here, is that understood? If I so much as hear an inkling of your name in these cases apart from your witness status I will charge you with obstruction, is that clear?'

Matilda nodded her head, 'Totally inspector.'

'Good! Now I'll bid you good day,' and he turned on his heels and strode out of the pub.

Silence, then aunt picked up the phone and dialled a London number. Sylvia answered after the first ring.

'Good morning Sylvia. I've a little job for you if you're not too busy.'

I left aunt to it, and wandered through the conservatory to the back garden of the pub, which gently sloped down to the river.

A favourite place of mine was a wooden bench nestled under a weeping willow tree; so old and bent, the branches formed a bridge that almost reached the other side of the bank. Peaceful, soothing, serene were the adjectives that sprung to mind as I sat, legs stretched out in front of me, idly watching a king fisher darting backwards and forwards, hunting small fish inhabiting the slow moving river.

Murder…

How could murder be a part of this idyllic scene? This was my home, my sanctuary ever since I was six years old when aunt threw her doors and her heart open to a bewildered little girl whose life had changed in an instance when her parents were killed in a car crash on the motorway.

I stirred restlessly on the bench.

Even though it all happened nearly twenty years ago, I knew I would never forget that initial feeling of devastation enveloping me when aunt told me what had happened to my lovely parents. Dad was aunt's baby brother and my mum, well, she looked upon as a sister, so the two of us mourned our lost loved ones together and somehow we got through it. I did well at boarding school, enjoying the structured life which I needed for the stability it gave; whilst at the same time enabling aunt to continue with her career, gallivanting all over the place, except during school holidays.

Those were sacrosanct.

We had the most wonderful times together; exploring out of the way places untrodden by tourists but known to aunt courtesy of her formidable list of contacts she'd built up over the years. My love of archaeology developed during those formative years of discovery, museums and art galleries my stomping grounds, ancient Greece and Egypt my motivation. There was no more enthusiastic student than I on my first day at uni, and then five years later collecting my Master's degree. Aunt had always encouraged me to challenge myself so, back to the books to get my PhD.

I was fortunate to be picked by Professor Philips to join his team whilst at the same time able to continue studying. Everything looked very rosy on the horizon until now.

I could understand aunt's outrage at such a horrific event happening in our lovely home. Defiled was putting it politely as far as I was concerned. How dare anybody do such a thing! But of course, guilt was playing heavily on my mind as I was the one who had somehow unknowingly lured Philip Westbury to this neck of the woods. Damn him!

'You shouldn't speak ill of the dead,' said Aunt Matilda, as she sat next to me.

'Sorry. I didn't realise I said it aloud.'

'Anyway, I've something to tell you. Sylvia has come up trumps as usual. Philip Westbury and Frederick Short are related. They are or were uncle and nephew. Swingen Linen isn't in the picture as yet; Sylvia's still working on that. This affair gets more interesting by the minute. Let's have breakfast whilst we discuss this latest development.'

To be honest, I wasn't enthusiastic like aunt, in fact the opposite. I was more concerned about our well-being. There must be a lot at stake if someone was willing to kill so cold bloodedly and take the chances he or they were taking.

But I was sure I could keep a check on aunt's enthusiasm.

THE INTRIGUE DEEPENS.

We ate breakfast in the pub's conservatory.

Even though it was Monday, there wasn't the usual hustle and bustle in the air heralding the start of the working week, even by the Bubbling Brook. Matilda's village was too far off the beaten track to even hear a faint rumble of traffic.

Lounging in our chairs as the sun's rays danced on the river, listening to birds chirping, and watching swallows doing aerobatics in their quest for breakfast, everything so peaceful and tranquil, again it seemed impossible anything as brutal as murder could happen in such heavenly surroundings.

'A phone call for you, Matilda,' called Bob, the pub's proprietor through the open door.

Aunt disappeared and then returned in a couple of minutes.

'That was the inspector. We can return home. The police have finished everything they need to do.'

It didn't take us long to gather our belonging and soon we were back at the cottage.

OK, I'll admit we both seemed to deliberately steer clear of the lounge, although the only evidence of wrongdoing was a wet patch on the carpet where Philip's blood had oozed and some kind soul had cleaned it up.

Nonetheless, we made a beeline to the kitchen, put on the kettle and then sat quietly at the table waiting for it to boil.

Aunt Matilda spoke.

'I've been thinking about that name Makokoshla. I'm convinced it has something to do with Africa. Why don't I just Google it and see what happens?'

'Good idea. While you do that, I think I'll concentrate on the fax and printout. Maybe I can figure out what they mean. It will give me something to do anyway,' and aunt gave me the papers she stored in her carpetbag.

She then disappeared to the office in her bedroom.

Meanwhile, I sat at the kitchen table with pencil, paper, eraser and two pages of jumbled letters and numbers. I tried everything I could think of to see what message, if any, there was to decipher. I juggled the vowels, ran rings around the xyz's, and played with the consonants. The fax and printout were not identical, but it seemed obvious the same key was needed to open both. Frustration was rapidly gaining the upper hand.

Then I heard a triumphant whoop before aunt clattered down the stairs waving a bundle of letters.

'From the sound of it, you've got lucky. I gather you've found a reference to Makokoshla?'

'It's a gold mine!'

'A what?'

'A gold mine in Africa. Or, at least it was many years ago, but whether it's still in operation after all this time I really don't know. The name came up on the computer but with very little info except it's in the midlands area of Zimbabwe in central Africa. But I was still sure I knew the name from somewhere, so, I hunted for letters from friends and acquaintances in Africa and found these written to my parents, your grandparents, Louise and Neville, that I kept all these years as I didn't have the heart to throw away when they died. They've been stuck in an old hat box forever. They were written by a friend who I think passed away at least forty years ago. He was a good mate of my father.

Your grandmother was a young bride when she first met him in Kenya after going there on safari with your grandfather. I can vaguely remember father talking about him, something to do with prospecting, I think, but what is amazing, and really is something I shouldn't have forgotten, is his surname was Westbury, Arthur Westbury,'

For once I was speechless.

This very old friend of my grandparents had the same surname as Philip who just happened to get murdered in this cottage! How bizarre!

'We must sift through these letters to see if Arthur Westbury mentions having a family and find out more about the mine, and who knows what else.'

Matilda was like a bloodhound; hence her very successful business.

The hunt was on!

She settled herself at the kitchen table, divided the letters in half and said, 'you go through those and make notes of anything interesting or unusual you come across. I'll do the same with these. That way we shouldn't miss anything.'

We soon became engrossed in what we were reading.

HIDDEN DEEPLY.

In November 1910, Arthur Westbury planned a prospecting expedition to the Zimbabwe Midlands. Over the years he'd heard mention of an old gold mine buried deep in the bushveld, which had the mysterious name of Makokoshla.

Arthur was determined to find it.

He visited the mining offices in the various towns of the Midlands, hunting down old maps to see if this mine was mentioned in any of the ordinance surveys. No mention was to be had. However, he found out from the locals that the name Makokoshla was a Mashona tribal word meaning 'hidden deeply.'

Deciding a systematic search of the area between the town of Selukwe and the Midlands capital of Gwelo was necessary; Arthur organized an expedition party, and departed at the end of January 1911, on foot, trekking in the bush. Food wasn't a problem, as there was plenty of game to be had, and by necessity, Arthur was an excellent shot.

However, he wrote regarding accidents befalling his bearers until it reached the stage when, after three months, the bearers that were left refused to go any further. Being very superstitious, they agreed amongst themselves the journey was displeasing to their ancestral spirits and more accidents would occur if they continued. They downed tools, and returned to their homes. Arthur had no choice but to do the same.

Nevertheless, by speaking to the locals he met on the way, he was informed about a huge fig tree growing by the mine. (This was interesting, as fig trees are not indigenous to Zimbabwe, so how did one start growing in the middle of the bush?)

Nothing daunted, Arthur set up another expedition in January 1913, and apparently found the mine. The information he wrote around this time was very scanty, although he did mention the fig tree but the main news he was concerned about was how imminent the First World War was, and that was the last letter Louise and Neville received. 'I'm sure they thought he'd been killed in the war,' said aunt.

'He hasn't made mention of having a family. It's strange his letters end on finding the mine. I wonder if there's any significance in that.'

'It does seem odd Arthur's letters stopping around that time. Don't you see, Ella? Maybe this whole thing started way back in 1913 when Arthur found that mine. Makokoshla is the key. I'm certain of it.'

'I think you might be letting your imagination run away with you, aunt. That mine was found over ninety years ago.'

'But listen. Isn't it strange that two of Arthur's relatives have been murdered and the name Makokoshla has suddenly surfaced after all this time, and that one of the murders happened here? Did Philip Westbury know our family was acquainted with his long lost relative?'

Aunt had a point.

'So, what do you intend doing with this information?'

'Well, what say we go to Zimbabwe and see if we can find the mine? No, wait before you start objecting you're on holiday for at least six weeks. I'm supposed to be retired and frankly, I'm getting pretty bored, so why not have a holiday in Africa. I don't think for a minute we'll find anything but it will be fun trying, and anyway, Inspector Stuart seems quite adamant that the fax has nothing to do with the murders.'

Although Aunt Matilda's suggestion seemed preposterous at first, the more I thought about it, the more appealing it sounded. We always had great times exploring new places together, and this trip sounded exotic, and, of course, my archaeological background may come in handy so, hunting for a gold mine in the middle of the African bush, what better way to spend a holiday?

Then common sense took over.

'You do realise if we've come to this conclusion, the murderer is probably thinking the same? And what about Inspector Stuart? I'm sure we have to hang around for inquests or whatever. Have you forgotten we are involved up to our eyeballs?'

Aunt Matilda thought for a moment.

'Well, we'll manage one way or another, I'm sure. There's a lot to organise Ella. We must phone the airlines and see if there is a direct flight to Zimbabwe. We need to organize anti-malarial tablets, book our flight, pack for warm climes and go on a treasure hunt looking for a gold mine!'

OFF ON A JOURNEY.

I have always been in awe of Matilda's organizing abilities but this time she surpassed herself.

At Philip Westbury and Frederick Short's inquests, which took place two weeks after their murders, the verdicts were killed by person or persons unknown and both were postponed pending further investigations. Matilda worked her magic with Inspector Stuart who appeared to have no problem with us continuing with our holiday plans as long as the police had all our personal details including mobile phone numbers so we could be contacted at any time. Somehow, aunt gave the impression these plans had been in the pipeline for quite a while without actually saying so.

I telephoned Professor Philips and gave him an abbreviated brief on what had occurred. He told me to take as long as I needed to get things sorted.

Tickets for the flight to Harare, the capital of Zimbabwe were booked, anti-malarial tablets swallowed, bags packed, travellers cheques bought, passports checked, and within ten days of the inquests we were in my car heading for London and Heathrow Airport.

I had the fax and printout in my hold all.

We arrived at Heathrow the stipulated three hours before the flight, and after parking the car in the long-term car park, checked in our luggage, and then spent the rest of the time discussing our itinerary once we arrived in Zimbabwe.

I had an International Driving License, so hiring a car and driving to the Midlands capital of Gweru was first priority.

Our flight was called, and after stowing our hand luggage, we settled ourselves, hoping to get as much sleep as possible, as we had a long journey ahead of us.

We arrived at Harare International Airport at twenty past six the next morning.

The weather was absolutely glorious!

Even at that time in the morning, the sun was shining with such clarity, all images appeared sharper. There wasn't the fuzzy look that often hovers over the English sun.

It didn't take long to get through passport control, pick up our luggage and make our way to the nearest Avis Car Rental. After exchanging travellers' cheques for Zimbabwean dollars, we hired an Avis rental and bought several maps, a large one of the country as a whole, and a smaller one of the streets of Harare, plus a street map of Gweru.

'Do you feel like driving to Gweru today, Ella, or would you prefer we spend the day in Harare and drive through tomorrow?'

'I wouldn't mind having a look around the capital, aunt. We could put up at a hotel just for tonight and feel refreshed for tomorrow. I've never managed to sleep well on planes.'

And that's what we did.

We drove near the city centre and found a secluded hotel called The Flamboyant, tucked away in a beautiful tree lined avenue. After unpacking the few necessities we would need, we set off to explore this beautiful city.

What struck my eye immediately was the enormous number of trees lining the wide avenues of Harare. They were Jacarandas, covered in beautiful lilac blossom, which carpeted the roads and pavements

'Those large umbrella shaped trees in-between the Jacarandas are called Flamboyants. They have fiery orange blossoms, which come out after the Jacaranda blossoms pass. It's a glorious sight, eh Ella?'

I nodded as I adjusted my camera. I was never able to exactly reproduce the colour of those blossoms on film.

The hawkers, selling their wares on the roadside, had goods ranging from mangoes to intricately carved wooden figures and animals, all there to tempt eye and purse.

I could easily have forgotten we weren't tourists on a carefree holiday, but instead, were involved in something far more serious.

England seemed very remote. I just wanted to soak up the blazing sun, explore this magnificent country with its breath-taking scenery and forget such things as double murders, faxes and printouts.

We had a leisurely dinner at the hotel; king prawns, always a favourite indulgence, and then tucked into a luscious fresh fruit salad of paw paw and mango for dessert.

Whilst sipping the best freshly ground coffee I'd ever tasted, we discussed our next plan of action.

'We must visit the Commissioner of Mines,' said Matilda. 'I know they have offices in all the mining areas, so I'm sure there's one in Gweru. Maybe we can get some geological maps from somewhere, showing mines and mine workings. They may even have old maps dating back ninety years plus. It's worth a try anyway. Have you finished your coffee? Let's make an early night of it. Breakfast at seven and then we hit the road.'

After a restful sleep and a good bacon and egg breakfast, we were bowling along the road towards Gweru before eight the next morning.

AFRICA.

Gweru is approximately 200 miles from Harare.

The road was well maintained, making driving a pleasure. We drove through grassland stretching to infinity.

Now and again large outcrops of granite rock loomed on either side of the road, huge boulders doing a balancing act on top of one another where the softer sandstone had weathered away.

Clusters of huts with thatched roofs dotted the landscape, many brightly painted with geometric designs. Small fields of mealies were planted by each hut, protected by prickly pear trees growing in abundance.

Now and again we came across large tracts of land under cultivation, with farmhouses nestling under towering blue gum trees interspersed with Jacarandas and Flamboyants giving plenty of shade.

The sun shone as brilliantly as ever, the contrasting shadows appearing even blacker and sharper than in Harare, a painter's paradise. Being totally inartistic, I envied those people who were able to dab a few splodges of paint on canvas and come up with a masterpiece.

Halfway through our journey, we stopped at a welcoming motel called appropriately, The Oasis. It was literally in the middle of nowhere.

We had a long cool drink of guava juice whilst sitting under a brightly coloured umbrella, overlooking the bluest swimming pool I had ever seen. Whether it was the reflection of the sun and blue sky on the water, I don't know, but the pool was truly dazzling.

'Next stop Gweru, Ella. Shall we be on our way before it gets too late?'

I reluctantly dragged myself away from this tranquil setting.

'Why so quiet, Ella? Not like you at all.'

'Just thinking what lies ahead of us. I'm enjoying this trip so much it's easy to forget the real reason why we're here. I suppose when we get to Gweru, our first stop will be finding a bed for a few nights. Then we should hunt down the mining commissioner's office and get hold of some geological maps of the area.'

The rest of the journey passed quickly.

The Meikles Hotel was the main one in Gweru, built on colonial lines, with a white and cream façade and luxurious interior. A dazzlingly white uniformed porter, black skin in startling contrast, showed us to our rooms. These were decorated in indigenous style with animal skins on the walls and floors and intricately carved bedside lamps and headboards. The desk and chest of drawers had carved wooden relief depicting scantily clad maidens carrying large water containers on their heads walking to the river. Animals abounded in the carvings with plenty of fauna and flora filling in the gaps. The carvings were done in a dark attractive wood called Meranti. They were amazingly intricate and I was studying them carefully when Matilda walked into the room.

'Come on Ella! Plenty of time to look at all that later. Let's get tracking Makakoshla,' and she dumped her carpet bag on the one item in the room I didn't fancy, a side table made out of a stuffed elephant's leg and foot, complete with toe nails. It was gross!

We made enquiries at the reception desk as to the whereabouts of the mining commissioner's office. The helpful receptionist gave clear directions, and soon we were parked outside a one-story building, complete with veranda. Wrought iron work painted in emerald green surrounded the veranda, contrasting nicely with the khaki coloured walls and black roof. A highly polished brass sign proclaimed Jacob Muller as Gweru's official mining commissioner.

We climbed the steps leading to the veranda and knocked on the emerald green painted wooden door. This was opened by an elderly African man, smartly dressed in khaki shirt and shorts with long beige socks covering two spindly legs ending in a pair of highly polished brown boots.

We were ushered into an office which had the absolute bare essentials: one desk, one chair, a couple of filing cabinets and a calendar on the wall printed by the Mashona Mining Company. The other walls were covered in geological maps.

Mr. Muller, the mining commissioner, was sitting at his desk writing, but looked up sharply as we made quite a racket on the wooden floors.

Two chairs were brought into the office, and we were politely requested to take a seat.

Aunt Matilda did the introductions and requested a look at any old maps the commissioner may have of the area, and maybe an up to date one we could purchase.

Whilst aunt prattled on, I took stock of the commissioner.

He was very tall and lean, probably in his mid-thirties, with not an ounce of flab on him. But what really caught my attention were his eyebrows. They were as black as his mop of curly hair, and triangular in shape, the apex of the triangles pointing directly to his forehead. When he frowned, which he was now doing constantly, he had a definite satyr look about him. He was unquestionably very attractive, but of course, I was totally immune.

Aunt ground to a halt.

The commissioner regarded her out of almost black eyes and finally said,' I believe I can help if you wouldn't mind going into the next office. We have maps dating back to the turn of the century when explorers from Europe and England were visiting the continent.'

We followed the commissioner next door, and entered a room filled with rows of racks with maps folded over them. Each set of racks had dates attached that made for easy reference.

'What time period were you interested in, Miss Stanbridge?'

I turned to see the commissioner regarding me with those piercing black eyes.

'Well, around 1940 onwards would be a good place to start if you have any going back that far. We had heard mention of an old mine with the peculiar name of Makokoshla. I believe it was worked round about that time.'

Commissioner Muller's eyebrows became even more pronounced as he studied me carefully for a moment.

Was it my imagination that the not so congenial atmosphere froze up even more?

However, he turned on his heels and strode towards the racks in the far corner of the room.

Pointing to dates reading 1900 to 1930, he said, 'these are copies of maps from that time. You can examine them and see if what you are looking for is there. If you need later dates, the maps are placed in chronological order around the room this way,' and swept his sun burnt arm towards the right.

'The originals are locked away in cabinets because of their fragility. I shall be in my office if you need any further assistance,' and with that parting shot, he strode out of the office in all his khaki finery and closed the door onto his own.

'I wouldn't say he was the friendliest person I have met,' said Matilda, looking at the closed door with a frown on her face. She shrugged and then turned to the job at hand.

We took out the geological map of the Gweru area, dated 1900, and spread it on a large wooden table conveniently placed in the middle of the room.

'I'll start at this end and you begin at the other and let's see if we come across any name that looks like Makokoshla. I'm glad I brought my magnifying glass with me. These names are written in tiny letters,' and Matilda dived into her carpetbag and pulled out a Sherlock Holmes.

She bent over the map, muttering to herself as she read off the names of various places and landmarks. I went to my side and ran my eyes up and down the grids, hunting for any clue that might lead to the whereabouts of the mine.

Nothing appeared even remotely similar to the name.

'Didn't you mention a town called Selukwe? Let's see if we can find it and concentrate our search in that area. I'm sure Selukwe or Sekerie as it's now called is fairly close to Gweru.'

'Good idea Ella. I'd forgotten that bit of information.'

We bent over the map again.

Sure enough, there was Selukwe, situated, according to the map, about thirty miles from Gweru. Unfortunately, the name Makokoshla was nowhere to be seen.

'Well, it would have been amazing if we'd stumbled upon it first go. Let's look at some later maps and see if we get lucky,' and Matilda strode over to the rack dated 1940 to 1955.

While I was putting the one we'd been looking at back in its rightful place, she spread the later one on the table and bent over it, magnifying glass in hand again.

'Bingo!'

OUT IN THE STICKS.

I leaned over to see where Matilda was pointing her finger.

'That looks like a farm with the name Makoshla. It's just missing the middle bit. It could well be connected to the mine with the middle bit removed to differentiate the two. I'll get out the latest maps and compare them with this one. After all, many years have passed since this one was drawn up.'

There was no mention of the farm on the later maps. Working backwards, we found the last mention of Makoshla on a map dated 1951. After that, nothing.

'We must write down the co-ordinates of the farm from the 1951 map. Then we get ourselves an up to date one and plot where the farm would have been if it were still in existence. At least that will give us some idea where to start looking for the mine. Who knows, maybe that fig tree is still standing like a beacon,' and I scribbled down the co-ordinates in my diary.

We knocked on the commissioner's door to thank him for his help and asked if he had an up to date map we could buy.

'Reuben!' called the commissioner.

The commissioner's assistant came running.

'Please get these ladies a geological map of the Midlands.'

Once that was purchased, we said our goodbyes and went out into the blinding sun.

'Thank goodness I parked under some shade. The car would've been like an oven standing in the sun. What shall we do next? Go mine hunting?'

'I'm not sure taking this car into the bush would be a good idea, aunt. Maybe we should try and hire a land rover or something similar. One of those 4 wheeled drive vehicles would be more suitable.'

We drove back to the hotel and asked our friendly receptionist where we could hire a vehicle that could withstand the rigours of the bushveld. We were directed to the Midlands Garage situated next door to the town hall. The town clock chimed twelve as we drove out of the garage in a land rover; ideal for rough terrain.

'Let's eat lunch at that restaurant across the road, Ella. We'll sit at one of the pavement tables.'

Whilst munching on dishes of delicious exotic fruit salads, we reviewed the situation.

I felt we had made reasonable progress considering the little we had to go on.

After plotting the co-ordinates of the farm on our map, I studied the layout. We had to take the main road leading east out of Gweru and about a third of the way to Sekerie, take a left turn onto a dirt road and keep driving until it forked. The farm would have been situated between the two forks if it had still existed.

'That looks pretty easy to find,' said Matilda, after I pointed out where on the map Makoshla would've been.

'Have you finished eating your salad? Good. Let's get going.'

Aunt Matilda paid our bill as I collected our belongings.

We found the road leading to Sekerie, and drove along it for about ten miles until I saw a signpost on the left pointing to Chavamba.

I stopped the land rover and consulted the map.

As I bent my head to check I had the correct turning, a grey BMW slowed up behind us as if to stop, and then overtook quickly. For some reason, I felt slightly uneasy.

Matilda, impatient as ever, shook my shoulder and told me to wake up! Is this the right road or not?

'Looks like it aunt. We'll drive along it until we get to the fork in the road and then have a look around.'

Although a dirt road, it was well maintained. The width was wide enough to allow three cars to travel abreast. The road was so smooth, regular grading must have taken place. Either side was fenced, although no crops had been planted. The land was obviously used for grazing purposes.

'How far along do we travel before we get to the fork?' I asked Matilda, as she had commandeered the map.

'Looks like about six miles as the crow flies. We should be coming to it quite soon at the rate we're travelling.'

Driving around the next bend, there was the fork. We slowed to a halt and I parked off the road by a gate. We had driven into a valley, and on both sides rose steep hills with many rocky outcrops, ideal terrain for troops of baboons.

Silence enveloped us or so it seemed.

We sat for a few minutes savouring the African bush. The silence was actually deceiving. There was a constant hum from myriads of insects; above that was the trill and shrills of many birds and over that noise was the sound of animals, the loud bark of baboons being the most prevalent.

'You do know where there is baboon; leopard is also to be found lurking,' said Matilda in a mock stage whisper.

I grinned at her and threw my camera strap around my neck, pocketed the land rover keys and walked the few hundred yards to where the Makoshla farmhouse was supposed to have been standing.

Of course, after all this time, there was really nothing to see. Any remains of buildings that might have existed had long been claimed back by the bushveld.

'Wouldn't it be great if the mine is around here somewhere. However, if it hasn't been worked for fifty years plus, how on earth are we going to find it?' said aunt, trudging over the rocky ground to stand beside me.

'I've an idea that's been simmering in the back of my mind ever since we went to the mining commissioner.

The fax and printout are a jumble of letters and numbers making no sense at all. Maybe there are grid references amongst them and maybe, just maybe, if we find the grid reference that we have for this farm amongst them, we'll have a starting point to go on.'

'Good thinking, Ella. It's certainly worth a try.'

I went back to the land rover and unlocked the door to get my bag from behind the front seat. Tucked away in one of the zipped pockets, were the fax and printout.

I gave the fax to aunt whilst I studied the printout, and within a minute I had found what I was looking for. The grid reference for the farm was staring at me almost accusingly. It looked so obvious, but that's always the case once you know what you are looking for.

'Here's the grid reference, aunt. Now, all we have to do is compare the printout and the map for any other grid references and see where it leads us.'

It would take us deep into the rocky overgrown terrain leading up from the valley.

'If my calculations are correct, the mine should be somewhere between that huge outcrop of rock on the left,' and I pointed the way to Matilda, 'and that very inhospitable looking piece of land towards the right.'

We both stood staring in the direction I'd pointed to and came to the same conclusion.

'Ella, we shall have to come back tomorrow, far more suitably dressed. That looks quite a trek, and we don't know how far the land rover will take us.'

CYANIDE?

Early the next morning we were driving back along the dirt road.

We'd made arrangements with the garage to hire the land rover for another day, and picked it up when they opened their doors at seven.

I was suitably dressed for hiking around the bush in shirt, jeans, sturdy walking boots and a bush hat. Even this early in the morning, the sun was pouring out a fierce heat. Matilda had donned a pair of voluminous culottes, a paisley patterned blouse and protecting her head, a fancy flowered print hat with a large brim. She was also sporting walking boots that looked a tad incongruous with the rest of her attire.

We made sure of a good supply of water plus a pack lunch so, hopefully, there was no stopping us finding the mine.

I'd looked carefully at the map the evening before, and noticed several tracks leading up into the hills the way we wanted to go. If we could find one of those tracks, I was confident the land rover could take us close to our eventual destination.

We reached the fork and stopped. I unfolded the map, spread it out on the bonnet of the land rover and showed aunt which track I thought we should follow to get as close to the x I'd marked where I guessed the mine should be.

'So, we take the left hand fork for about two miles, and then we should see a turn off on the left, leading up into the hills. We must take note of any landmarks on the way so we don't get lost. I wouldn't fancy being stuck out here at night.'

Aunt Matilda settled back into her seat and chuckled.

'I can't tell you how much I'm enjoying myself. Of course, I'm sorry about poor Philip Westbury and Mr. Short, but you have to admit it, Ella, this is far more exciting than being back at the village picking blackberries.'

I nodded in agreement, although I couldn't shake off a feeling of apprehension. It was nothing I could put my finger on, just a faint disquiet that events had been running a bit too smoothly and we were in for a shake-up.

After driving a couple of miles along the dirt road, I saw an opening in the bush. I turned left and followed the dirt track as it twisted and turned, first to the left, and then to the right. We kept this up for at least an hour, driving deeper and deeper into the bush, at the same time steadily climbing. Now and again we caught glimpses of baboons watching us for a few seconds before leaping into trees and disappearing from sight. Once I thought I saw a duiker run across the track ahead of us, but it was gone so quickly, I couldn't be sure if I'd seen it or not. The bushveld was getting so thick by this time I knew we would have to stop soon. Even a land rover would find it impossible to continue for much further. I found a small clearing and turned off the engine.

'We'll have to continue on foot, aunt. There's no way I can drive any further.'

I looked at the map again and decided a compass bearing of NNW would take us to the huge outcrop of rock I'd noticed yesterday.

After putting a couple of plastic water bottles in a small rucksack I'd brought along, plus our packed lunch, we used the compass to point us in the right direction and proceeded to plod through the bushveld.

It was hard going.

Although the thick bush sheltered us from the sun, the heat was stifling. Even the sound of insects was muffled.

We walked for over an hour and then I spotted a clearing ahead of us.

'This could be it!' I shouted excitedly.' How are you doing aunt? We could be there!'

'Considering my age, not bad at all,' she retorted. 'I must say though, I wouldn't mind having a rest soon and drinking some of that lovely water you're carrying.'

'If you didn't insist on lugging that carpetbag with you wherever you go, you would find the going much easier. It would've been safe, locked in the land rover.'

'Now, now Ella. You know me better than that. Of course I wouldn't leave my bag behind. The very thought.'

I helped Matilda up the last bit of animal track we'd been following, and then we both just stood, mesmerized by what we were seeing.

We had come out of the thick bush into a clearing surrounded on both sides by huge boulders. However, ahead of us was a view that stretched forever; large sweeps of undulating hills covered in masasa trees coloured in all the hues that brown and green could offer. The purple mauve blossoms of Jacarandas dotted the landscape in beautiful contrast. The deep blue of the cloudless sky made a perfect backdrop to this masterpiece that could only have been painted by a Divine Artist.

We lowered ourselves onto a couple of boulders and gazed our fill. I raised my camera, knowing that any photos I took would never do justice to such a magnificent sight.

Eventually said to aunt we would have to start moving as time was passing. I offered her a last sip of water before checking the map again.

'Right. This is where we are, and this is where the mine should be,' and I ran my finger from where the outcrop of boulders were, and then towards the east and stopped halfway in-between.

'Let's follow the compass bearing east and see if my calculations are correct.'

Matilda eased herself up from the boulder she'd been sitting on.

'All my joints have stiffened up,' she complained, as she slowly walked along the track again.

I was getting concerned about her, but knew from past experience to suggest she was getting too old for this sort of thing would have brought untold wrath upon my head. I decided if we didn't find the mine in the next hour, I would tell her I was too tired to carry on and that tomorrow we would come back again. At least we would know where not to look, and aunt would 'save face.'

Following the compass bearing east, we plunged deep into the bush again. I noticed a gradual change in the type of rock littering the track.

'My geology is pretty rusty, but isn't gold found in quartz bearing rock?'

Matilda nodded her head in agreement.

'I remember seeing a small nugget of gold in quartz at a friend's house once. He collected samples of rock from all over the world. There were spectacular examples of amethyst in his collection as well.'

We continued walking for another thirty minutes and found ourselves stepping into a clearing that was definitely man made.

We stopped and looked around.

'This could well be it, Ella,' said aunt, voice quivering with excitement.

We were standing in an area about three hundred yards square. It had been stripped bare of any vegetation; the ground hard packed where numerous feet had stomped over it.

To the left were remains of wattle and daub huts, now reduced to uneven mounds of red clay, and to the right, three concrete reservoirs, two on the same level, and a deeper one built about ten foot lower than the other two. The top reservoirs were about fifteen foot in diameter and six foot deep. The bottom one was smaller but deeper. On closer inspection, I could see the remains of pipe work connecting the reservoirs together.

I saw a piece of weathered board hanging haphazardly from a post. Lifting it back into position, I could just make out the skull and crossbones. I then realised what we were looking at.

'This was a gold mine all right, aunt. At least, someone was busy leaching gold from the waste sand that had been brought up from the mine. You see this sign over here? It has a skull and crossbones painted on it. That was to warn everyone poison was being used. And guess what that poison was?'

Aunt Matilda shook her head, mystified.

'Cyanide'

'Cyanide? Why on earth would anybody want to use cyanide in gold mining?'

'I remember reading an article on how there was a lot of gold left in the gold bearing rock even after it had been crushed and the gold extracted, especially in the older mines, where the extraction processes were not very efficient. It was found that if a cyanide solution was passed through the gold bearing sand, any gold was dissolved in the solution. Then, the cyanide solution with the gold was passed through zinc shavings, and voila, the gold precipitated out onto the zinc shavings. A wash of the zinc in an acid solution loosened the grey sludge that had the gold in it, which was then smelted and you would be left with a button of gold.'

It felt good showing off my knowledge.

'Well, how about that,' said Matilda.

I had a look at some square metal tanks lying on their sides not far from the reservoirs, and deduced these were the tanks that had held the zinc shavings.

'Yes, we are definitely on the right track. Now, I wonder where the actual mine is. It can't be too far away because of the sands being treated here.'

'It would be very nice if we could find some way of verifying this is Makokoshla.'

'You have it, aunt. Look over there,' and Matilda turned to where I was pointing.

'My goodness! What a huge fig tree! Look how thick the trunk is. This must surely be the fig tree poor Arthur mentioned in his letter.'

It was huge and very, very old. I was absolutely amazed the tree was still standing, let alone bearing fruit. We moved closer to get a better look.

'I must take a photo of it, aunt. Go and stand by it so I can show just how big it is.'

Matilda stood leaning against the tree, looking admiringly up into its branches.

'Have you taken your picture yet Ella? I'm getting a stiff neck,' and Matilda turned to face me.

I was standing still as a statue.

Once I felt the cold steel of a gun barrel pressed against my temple, all desire to go on clicking had left me.

'Oh my goodness!' gasped Matilda, and she started to come towards me.

'I suggest you stay right where you are,' said my assailant. 'Ken! Get hold of the aunt and tie her up,' and out from behind a huge boulder came a large set man with a receding hair line, bulbous nose and a very unpleasant sneer on his face.

'I'm sure you wouldn't like to see your niece with a nice round hole in her head.'

'Just like Philip Westbury and Mr. Short,' retorted Matilda furiously, and then clapped her hands over her mouth as she realised that was the last thing she should have said.

'You catch on very quickly,' replied my assailant, and with the gun still pressed to my head, took me by the arm and pulled me towards the edge of the clearing where wooden planks were laid side by side. I was pushed to the ground, and my hands and feet tied with thin cord. Poor Aunt Matilda was afforded the same treatment, and the pair of us ended up looking like two trussed turkeys.

My assailant and Ken moved the planks away from the ground to reveal a large gaping hole. We were then half dragged, half carried to the edge of the hole.

'This is where we say goodbye, ladies,' and Matilda and then myself were pushed over the edge.

Down, down, down we fell.

It is absolutely true that when you face certain death, one's life does pass in front of one's eyes and everything appears to happen in slow motion. My first thought was I'd be seeing mum and dad again, my second, and I felt really sad about this, no one will ever find our bodies.

And then I hit the bottom of the shaft, but, although winded, I was, amazingly, still alive! And going by the soft groans near me, so was Matilda!

But how?

I realised, with amazement, we must have landed on an incredibly thick pile of assorted debris thrown down this particular shaft as a sort of waste disposal unit. The debris had built up over the years, a lot decaying and softening into a thick, very smelly organic cushion. To me, Chanel Number 5 could not have smelt any more fragrant.

Before I had time to assimilate our momentous escape from death, my haversack and aunt's carpet bag joined us, presumably to remove any evidence we had been at the mine.

Then, what little light we had was removed abruptly as the planks were put back in place, leaving us in total darkness.

LEFT FOR DEAD.

'Aunt! Are you alright?' I said softly, worried Ken and his accomplice might hear. They wouldn't have been so quick to throw us down the mine if they thought we had a chance of surviving.

'Well, for a sixty three year old, trussed up like a turkey, having been unceremoniously dumped down a mine shaft, I am as well as can be expected,' she replied tartly out of the darkness.'

I immediately felt my spirits rise.

One thing about my Aunt Matilda, she will never admit defeat.

'The first thing we must do is untie ourselves. If you can get hold of my bag, Ella, I know there's a pair of scissors and a small torch tucked away in one of the pockets.'

'They threw the bag and haversack down after us, so they can't be too far away. I'll shuffle around a bit until I find it.'

I wriggled around the area where I was lying, and after coming into contact with some very hard rocks, I finally felt something soft near my feet.

'I've found it aunt. Now all I have to do is get it near my hands. It would be much easier if I hadn't had them tied behind my back.'

Whilst talking, I'd managed to manoeuvre the bag so I could open the catch with my fingertips. Once opened, the problem was delving into its cavernous depths to locate the scissors.

'Have you any idea where they are? I could be hunting for ages amongst all the paraphernalia you keep in your bag.'

'It's in a side pocket, the one with the zip.'

I managed to grasp the zip fastener with my fingertips and pulled it open. The scissors were there. The next problem was to hold them in such a way the blades could cut the cord that bound my hands tightly together.

It wasn't easy.

By the time the last thread of cord was cut, my shoulders were screaming in agony, and I could feel beads of sweat running down my neck and dripping off my nose. If it hadn't been for Matilda's encouragement, I think I would have given up.

Once the cords were cut, the blood rushed back into my hands, causing such pain I sobbed aloud. After rubbing them for a few minutes to get some life into them, I delved into the bag again and rummaged for the small torch Matilda said was in another pocket.

Once found, I switched it on and swung it around to look at aunt, who'd gone unnaturally quiet.

She was about six feet away, lying on her side with her eyes closed. There was a large gash over her left eyebrow.

'Hang in there, aunt. I'll soon have you untied,' and after loosening the cord around my feet, I quickly crawled towards her.

Once Matilda's hands and feet were untied, I gave her some sips of water from the filled water container we had left in my haversack. I used a very little of the water to gently wash the gash over her eye to clean the blood away, and although it needed stitches, looked quite respectable once I'd dressed it with a plaster Matilda always kept in her carpetbag.

To think I'd wanted her to leave that bag in the land rover. If she had listened to me, there's no doubt we would've ended up as a pair of corpses.

That could still happen, I thought, but obviously didn't say anything aloud.

Matilda perked up after drinking the water.

'You've made a wonderful start in getting us out of here, Ella!'

I gave her a hug.

'No aunt. It's you and your carpetbag that's so wonderful.'

We leant against the wall of the shaft to assess the situation. I switched off the torch to conserve the battery.

Aunt insisted we eat some of the chicken sandwiches left over from our pack lunch to boost our flagging energy, and although not a great deal had changed in our situation, things didn't look quite so bad.

'Those two thugs wouldn't have been so quick in throwing our belongings down after us if they'd known what was in them,' chuckled Matilda. 'Serves them right.'

'Well, we've got two choices in getting out. One, to try and climb back up the mine shaft or two, see if there is another way out.'

'I know I couldn't climb back up, Ella, but if you could, I'll stay here whilst you get help.'

I switched on the torch and played the beam of light on the walls of the shaft. They were smooth, too smooth to climb without climbing gear.

'I'd need a winch to get up there.'

I swung the torch around where we were sitting.

A yard or so from where Matilda had landed were coco pan tracks leading off into the darkness.

'If we follow the tracks, we might get lucky.'

'But surely they'll lead us deeper into the hill.'

'Yes, but don't forget such things as ventilation shafts. There's a big chance we'll come across one we can climb out, if it was dug at an angle instead of straight up. Have you any spare batteries for the torch?'

'Of course.'

We collected our belongings, and with me leading, followed the tracks meandering deeper and deeper inside the mine.

The usual paraphernalia of mine workings was strewn along the tunnel. Old shovels and picks lay broken and discarded. Rusty lamps hanging from the walls by stained pieces of wire bore silent testimony to the hustle and bustle of bygone years, when sweating men had toiled in this inhospitable terrain.

I picked up a coil of hemp rope lying near the track. Could come in handy.

We trudged along, the tram tracks turning sharply at times as the hewn out tunnel tracked the gold vein.

A rustling noise in the darkness accompanied by squeaking, gave away the whereabouts of rodents scurrying from us. I didn't even want to think of what else in the animal or reptile line could be lying in wait, ready to jump out at us.

'Ella, I'm going to sit for a few minutes. My feet are swelling where those nasty men tied them so tightly.'

'No problem, aunt. We can take a breather.'

Settling ourselves on an upturned coco pan that had been derailed, I nonchalantly swung the torch around, and the beam shone on the hand of a skeleton hanging over the edge of a coco pan tucked away in a corner of the tunnel.

Matilda heard my gasp of shock and looked to where the torch was pointing.

'Oh my goodness. Now what!'

We reluctantly made our way to this gruesome discovery.

I played the torch over the skeleton that was curled up in the coco pan, the knees almost touching the chin of the grinning skull. The skeleton was clothed in rotting cloth that could have been denim overalls with the remains of hob nailed boots hanging off the feet.

'Well, I could be totally wrong but don't you think it looks like this man was murdered? Look at the way the skull is smashed in just above the ear. This person was bludgeoned to death and then dumped in this coco pan.'

'What a terrible way to die, and to be left here all these years is just too horrible to think of,' and Matilda groped her way back to where we'd been sitting, and buried her head in her hands.

I put my arm around her shoulders and gave her a hug.

'Come aunt. We must get out of here. Those murderers need to be arrested before any more bodies are found, especially ours. I just wish I knew what was at the bottom of this mystery. Who knows! Maybe this skeleton could well be part of the puzzle.'

I helped Matilda to her feet.

We stumbled along the passage, willing to feel the tell, tell draught of fresh air that would show us we were by a ventilation shaft. The torch battery finally began to flicker, and I quickly exchanged it for the fresh one. I knew if we didn't reach a shaft soon, once that battery was flat, our chances of getting out would be negligible.

'Come on. Come on. Where are you,' I was muttering frantically, when… there it was, the draught of cool air being sucked down into the musty tunnel.

I swung the torch above me, and saw roots pushing their way through the roof, swaying gently in the breeze.

The excitement of the discovery sent a surge of adrenaline through me.

All feelings of pain and tiredness were forgotten as I clambered onto an upturned drum and pushed away the roots covering the entrance to the ventilation shaft.

'Our luck is holding,' I yelled in excitement. 'The shaft is running at an angle, and I can even see a pinpoint of light at the end. It's going to be a tight squeeze, but I know we can make it!'

'I never doubted it for one minute, Ella.'

And we both grinned at each other.

'Now, the first thing we must do is tie the rope around your waist, aunt. I can pull myself up into the shaft. You climb on the drum, hand me your bag and the haversack, then I'll pull you up.'

I found an old wooden box, which I placed on the drum, and dragged myself into the shaft. It was about four foot square, making manoeuvring a little difficult, but once I had the bags safely stowed, it was quite easy bracing my legs and giving Matilda a good yank.

She'd always been lightly built, so pulling her into the shaft didn't present too much difficulty. I grasped her under the armpits and soon we were both crouching in the tunnel on all fours, ready to crawl to the light beckoning us.

Pushing the carpet bag and haversack ahead of me, we slowly made our way to the surface, the widening light urging us on. On reaching the entrance, I pushed my head through the opening. It was protected by an overhanging rock.

Making sure our two friends weren't around; I pulled myself through and then turned to help Matilda.

Soon we were lying flat on our backs, savouring the fresh air and heady feeling of freedom!

'We did it, we actually did it,' Matilda said, over and over as though she still didn't quite believe it.

Looking up into the sky, I saw day light was fading fast. My watch had smashed in the mine, but I estimated we'd been down it for at least six hours. In the middle of Africa, twilight does not exist. One minute it's daytime, the next, night, just like someone switching off a light.

And that's how it happened.

'Looks like we'll be spending the night in the bush after all,' I remarked. 'We'll look for the land rover in the morning. Let's try and get ourselves as comfortable as we can, eat what's left of lunch and get some rest. I've a feeling tomorrow will bring a whole new set of problems.'

My last thought before drifting off into an exhausted sleep, was how the night sky of Africa was filled far more abundantly with stars than the night sky of England.

THE SWEET TASTE OF FREEDOM.

We woke to a beautiful morning.

To be honest, if it had been raining cats and dogs, we still would've thought it was beautiful. There's nothing like nearly losing one's life to put a different perspective on everything.

The sun was peeping over the hills; the barks of baboons already reverberating in the bush as they scavenged for breakfast, and the sound of numerous birds was music to our ears.

'I just need a nice cup of tea to make me feel totally human again,' said Matilda, and she slowly stretched her aching limbs.

'That and a delicious hot shower.'

I stood up and surveyed the scene.

We'd obviously emerged some distance from the mineshaft. I didn't recognize any landmarks from yesterday's journey.

Yesterday.

It seemed a lifetime ago. Did we really go through such a horrendous ordeal? One look at the plaster covering the gash over Matilda's eye assured me we had.

'You're developing quite a shiner, aunt. A pity you haven't a mirror so you can admire it yourself.'

'Oh, but I have, although it might've smashed when my bag was thrown down that dreadful shaft,' and she rummaged in the carpetbag.

'Good, it's only cracked,' and Matilda gently touched her eye whilst examining the damage.

'You don't look so hot yourself,' and she handed me the mirror, so I could look at my bruised and scraped face.

Not a pretty sight.

'I won't win any beauty contests, that's for sure, but the important thing now is to get to the land rover.'

I was confident if we could make our way to the large outcrop of rock we were at yesterday, it would be easy to back track to where the land rover was parked; if it was still there, that is.

I was hoping that as Ken and the other thug were waiting for us at the mine, they'd reached it by a different route. Okay! They could've found the vehicle and driven it away, but somehow, I didn't think so. Why not leave it where it was. Two inexperienced bush trekkers leaving their car to go traipsing in the bush could easily get lost and some natural disaster overtake them. Remember, leopards are always found in baboon country. No, I was sure they'd count on that line of thought being taken when the alarm was raised we were missing.

'We travelled east to get to the mine, so it stands to reason if we go west, we should be going in the direction of the outcrop. Do you feel up to another hike in the bush?'

'Lead the way, Ella. The sooner we tell the authorities about our encounter with those two monsters, the better,' and Matilda swung her carpetbag over her shoulder and stood there, waiting for me to 'lead the way.'

The compass had disappeared, but I made sure the rising sun's rays were kept warming our backs, which meant we were walking in a westerly direction.

It was slow going as our bodies had taken quite a beating yesterday, and the adrenaline rush I'd felt when finding the ventilation shaft had definitely subsided. Every bump and bruise was making itself felt.

The idea of a hot shower was becoming more appealing as we bruised ourselves clambering over rocks and the iniquitous thorn bushes tore at our skin.

The journey became easier when we stumbled on a track running in the right direction that was obviously used by small buck, going by the amount of droppings. One upsetting thing we saw were the remains of a small duiker with its head caught in a wire noose that had been rigged up over the track. The animal had run its head through the noose, which had tightened on its neck as it struggled to free itself and strangled it.

We battled on for what seemed like hours.

The sun was getting high in the sky, beating down on our heads with a merciless heat. A cool shower rather than a hot one was taking precedence in my mind.

Matilda had gone quiet.

I was sure the gash over her eye was throbbing, and with the sun shining brightly, she must be suffering from a blinding headache.

'Give me your bag, aunt. Let me carry it for a while. I bet it's feeling like a ton of bricks,' and I took it from her.

'Do you think we're nearly there, Ella? I must admit I'm flagging a little.'

'It can't be much further. It's hard to tell, as the bush looks the same wherever we go, but I'm sure I remember seeing that dead tree over to the right. Yesterday, there was a vulture perched on it.'

'I'm very relieved to see it's not there now. Don't vultures sense when something is about to die?' and we both laughed at that small snippet of macabre humour.

The outcrop of rock was eventually reached, and then it was easy going following the track back down the hill to where we had left the land rover.

Although I'd been pretty confident it would be there, I still felt a rush of relief when I saw it standing in the clearing. The feeling of relief was immediately replaced by worry that Ken and co had decided to sabotage it.

I had the keys tucked away in one of my jeans pockets. With trepidation I turned the starter motor over.

The land rover roared to life.

'Thank goodness for that,' I said elatedly and reversed the vehicle to go back down the hill towards the main dirt road, and then to Gweru.

'You know, Ella. There's something that's puzzling me. Something that just doesn't make any sense.'

'I think I know what you're going to say. Why didn't that goon shoot us when he had the chance? Our bodies could've been thrown down the mineshaft and that would have been the end of it.'

'Exactly! He shot Philip and Mr. Short without batting an eye. Why didn't he do the same to us? Who knows, maybe I reminded him of his mother, if a monster like that had one. Shooting women is not in his psyche, throwing them down a mine shaft is.'

We reached the end of the dirt road, and I was about to turn right, onto the tar, when I saw headlights flashing at us. A jeep skidded to a halt, and out jumped Jacob Muller, the mining commissioner.

He strode over to the land rover, opened my door and demanded to know where had we been all night!

JUSTIFICATION.

Matilda answered first.

'We were thrown down a mineshaft, and if it wasn't for my niece, we would still be there, probably dead!'

The commissioner looked at our battered appearances. His gaze zeroed in on the plaster over Matilda's left eye, which by now was puffed up and totally closed.

He turned to me. 'Are you able to follow me to the hospital? Your aunt needs medical attention to her eye, and your face, Dr Stanbridge, has seen better days. (Did he have to say that?) And then I have some questions I would like to ask.'

I turned to Matilda.

'Our knight in shining armour was a bit late in arriving, aunt. However, lead us to the hospital, commissioner.'

With a curt, 'Follow me,' he strode back to his jeep and within half an hour, I was in the casualty department of Gweru Hospital, waiting for the doctor to finish stitching the gash over Matilda's eye. X-rays showed nothing broken, which was a relief.

Meanwhile, the commissioner had driven to the Gweru Police Station and returned with Sergeant Ndlovu and two associates who took down our statements and promised to put the wheels of the law in motion.

After receiving anti tetanus injections, and a date for aunt to have her sutures removed, we left the hospital and were driven to the Meikles Hotel under police protection.

Sergeant Ndlovu drove to the Midlands garage to deposit the land rover and pick up our Jetta. Meanwhile, we enjoyed the shower that had dominated our thoughts, knowing two armed policemen were stood outside our hotel rooms.

Feeling, if not looking, nearly normal again, we were escorted to a private office where the commissioner was waiting for us at a table set for a meal.

He rose and pulled out our chairs.

Once we were settled, the commissioner said 'I took the liberty of ordering a pot of tea and scones for you. If you want something more substantial, that can be arranged.'

'That sounds perfect. Mr. Muller. We can eat a proper meal later,' replied Matilda.

Tea and scones arrived, and I busied myself playing mother.

During our visit to the hospital, Matilda had told the commissioner some of what had happened. She'd been deliberately vague in places, and the story sounded more as though we'd stumbled upon the mine by accident, and had no idea why anyone would want to kill us by throwing us down a mine shaft.

Jacob Muller was not easily fooled.

'Now, I really think you should start at the beginning, which means back in England to the first event that eventually led you to Zimbabwe and Gweru.'

There was silence.

Having nearly lost our lives had replaced the excited feeling of being on a treasure hunt, with an intense feeling of danger. This game was now deadly serious.

'Okay, Commissioner Muller. We'll fill you in from the time Aunt Matilda found a body in her cottage,'

That caught his attention!

Now and again, the commissioner interrupted to ask some pertinent question to clarify something that was said, but mostly he listened to our story, which sounded extraordinary even to our ears.

'Well, that's quite a tale you've told.'

There was a pause, then, 'Where did you hear the name Makokoshla?'

By unspoken consent, Matilda and I had left the fax and printout out of the narrative.

Aunt tried answering that question, and frankly, not very successfully.

'Well, we saw the name written on a piece of paper on Frederick Short's desk, and after finding out it was the name of a gold mine, decided to try and track it down. If we'd known the consequences of our innocent excursion, we would've stayed in England, wouldn't we Ella?'

'Absolutely.'

The commissioner looked at us in turn, his face inscrutable. He didn't question us further.

'Right now it's vital for those two individuals to believe they've succeeded in killing you. I can't think of any reason as to why they would want you dead, but as long as they think you are dead you won't be in any more danger. Therefore, I propose you come to my farm, which is on the outskirts of Gweru. It's quite secluded. I'm sure you'll be safe there until they're caught. I have already put this suggestion to Sergeant Ndlovu and he agrees with this plan.'

I looked at Matilda, who was about to object to this suggestion. There was no way I was going to allow her or myself for that matter, to embark on any more schemes that could seriously jeopardize our health. We'd pushed our luck to the limit. Next time could be our last.

'Thank you commissioner. We accept. I hope your wife won't mind having two strangers foisted on her?'

'Oh, I'm not married and please call me Jacob,' and the commissioner pushed back his chair and reached for mine.

'Oh, right, Jacob it is, then.'

'Now, I think we'd better get moving.'

TEVREDE.

It didn't take us long to pack.

Jacob, meanwhile, settled our account at reception. He put our suitcases in the back of the jeep and said, 'Sergeant Ndlovu will bring the Jetta to the farm.'

I climbed into the jeep first, followed by Matilda. The commissioner swung into the driver's seat and drove quickly away from the hotel.

We drove in the opposite direction to Sekerie.

After a couple of miles, Jacob turned sharp right, and once again we were driving on a wide dirt road. This carried on for several miles, the road flanked with huge fields of mealies. Now and again we could see cattle grazing in the distance.

'Is this part of the farm?' I asked Jacob.

'Yes. It's been in my family for five generations. We mainly farm beef and mealies as you can see. The farm is called Tevrede, which means satisfied in the Afrikaans language. You'll see the farmhouse as we go around the next bend.'

It was beautiful; a two storey building, built in the old colonial style with a veranda snaking around the perimeter. The house was painted white with wide shiny red steps leading up to the entrance. Flowers bloomed everywhere, many bordering a well-tended lawn. Jacaranda trees give plenty of shade; the largest having a wooden seat built around its trunk. Dark green iron wrought garden furniture clustered under another, and I could imagine sitting there, drinking a sundowner.

I heard a loud screeching noise as I followed Matilda up the steps, and turned quickly, to see a male peacock in all his glory, proudly strutting across the lawn.

I stared in amazement.

'They make very good watch dogs,' said Jacob, and took my elbow to lead me into the house.

Two employees, Gloria and her husband, Tazwhila, met us in the hallway, smiling as they welcomed us to Tevrede.

Our luggage disappeared, and Jacob suggested we unpack before having dinner at seven.

Matilda and I followed Gloria up the wide sweeping staircase, and were shown into adjoining bedrooms.

The time was six-thirty, so I quickly unpacked, and then went next door to Matilda's room.

She was lying on the bed, eyes closed as though she were sleeping. I tiptoed to the bed.

Aunt opened her eyes and said, 'I've a thumper of a headache. If the commissioner doesn't mind, I'm going to miss dinner tonight. I think the last couple of days have really caught up with me. I can tell you, Ella, I feel my age right now.'

'I'm sure he won't mind,' and helped aunt by unpacking her clothes.

'I'll ask Jacob if you can have a pot of tea and maybe a little soup in your room'.

I gently closed the bedroom door, and walked back down the staircase.

A door to one of the rooms opened, and out walked Jacob, khaki attire gone, and in its place, a white open neck shirt and grey flannels. He looked at me, his black eyes disconcertingly direct.

'Your aunt looked very tired when she went to her bedroom. Is she feeling alright, or should I send for the doctor?'

'I'm hoping she's just tired. She was complaining of a headache, so would it be possible for her to have a pot of tea and maybe a little soup in her room?'

'Of course. I'll organize it immediately.'

And Jacob turned tail and disappeared into the nether regions of the house, presumably to the kitchen.

I walked down the steps leading onto the lawn.

What could be called twilight in Africa was about to disappear in an instant.

As I made my way across the lawn to the garden chairs, the twinkling of a million stars suddenly appeared. The lights from the house cast pools of luminescence on the lawn, and I settled back in one of the chairs, whilst the nightlife of Africa came alive.

The noise of crickets was ever present, but now and again, I could hear the hoot of an owl, or some other night bird. Bats flew around the trees and darted towards the house, but what really caught my attention, was the overwhelming fragrance of blossom.

I wonder what flowers give off such a perfume at night, I thought, sniffing the night air.

'You are smelling Frangipani.'

Standing behind me was Jacob, carrying a tray with two glasses and a decanter. He settled the tray on the garden table, and poured a delicious looking drink into one of the glasses.

'Try this,' and the commissioner handed me the glass.

It tasted like nectar, a real blend of exotic fruits.

'It really is delicious. What's in it?'

'A mixture of mango, pineapple and Marula with a touch of spirit to give it a little bite. It's a concoction of Gloria's, but she won't tell me the exact combination. Family secret handed down through generations.'

I nodded, thinking of Matilda's blackberry pies. She did something to the pastry and filling which made them extra special, but it was impossible to get the recipe from her. She said she would leave the instructions for me in her will.

'I haven't heard of Marula. What is it?'

'Marula is a fruit that grows on trees. It's about the size of small plums and goes from green to yellow as it ripens. When ripe, the fruit falls off the trees and begins fermenting. There've been instances of monkeys and even elephants getting drunk on fermented marulas'

I laughed. I could picture in my mind a huge elephant swaying back and forth under the influence. I looked at my glass with new respect.

I'd better drink this slowly, I thought, mindful of my empty stomach.

Jacob poured some into the other glass, and settled himself in a chair opposite me.

'Your aunt is now enjoying chicken soup and sipping a traditional English cup of tea. She assures me she'll be as right as rain tomorrow, and that you mustn't worry about her, but just enjoy your dinner. That aunt of yours is a remarkable woman.'

Jacob glanced at me, his full lips smiling.

'It seems to run in the family. Dinner will be served in ten minutes, so you can bring your drink with you while we make our way to the dining room.'

I stood up from my chair and immediately felt slightly dizzy.

A touch of spirit! It's either the drink that's gone to my head, or the Frangipani blossom.

Jacob led me into the dining room.

The most dominant feature was a large mahogany table that could easily seat ten people. Two place settings had been arranged for us at one end of the table, facing each other. The cutlery was solid silver, and the crockery, porcelain.

I was stunned at the grandeur of it all.

'Do you always eat in such style?' I asked, whilst loosening a linen napkin from its silver napkin ring.

Jacob laughed.

'Gloria would so wish, but I must admit I usually eat in the kitchen when I'm alone. Having visitors has given her a golden opportunity to get out the best silver and chinaware. She loves having guests to stay. It gives her a chance to show off her culinary skills. She says I'm a very boring person to cook for, as I'm always happy eating pap and vleis.'

'Pap and vleis. What on earth is that?'

'Porridge and meat, with a tasty tomato gravy. I grew up on it, and have never tired eating it. I'm really the easiest person to cook for.'

Just then Tazwhila entered carrying a soup tureen.

'This looks like butternut soup. It's a popular African dish. I hope you enjoy it.'

'If the aroma is anything to go by, I'm sure I will.'

And I did.

Next on the menu was guinea fowl done in a fresh cream sauce, served with gem squashes and sweet potatoes. And if that wasn't enough, we had traditional melktart and koeksisters for desert, the koeksisters dripping in ice-cold syrup.

To help us swallow this delicious food, we drank wine cultivated from Jacob's own vineyard.

'We actually grow a limited quantity of an excellent table wine. We won a gold medal with this vintage, two years ago at the Annual Harare Wine Show,' he said with a certain amount of pride. 'I hope it isn't too dry for you?'

'It couldn't be more perfect. In fact, the whole meal was out of this world. I've never tasted anything like it. I must congratulate Gloria on her exquisite cooking.'

During the meal Jacob asked questions about my archaeological experiences.

'Most of my digs have been in Europe, Egypt and South America. This is the first time I've visited this continent, and apart from the unpleasant aspect of Ken and co, it really is an incredible place. The vastness of the country is breath-taking,' and I chattered on telling Jacob my impressions of the land of his birth.

He listened with an intensity I found flattering, and appeared interested in all I had to say, which made me even more eloquent, although the wine probably had something to do with that.

We finished the meal with freshly ground coffee and a variety of cheeses and savoury biscuits.

I leant back in my chair totally replete.

'It makes a refreshing change to find a female member of the human race who so heartily enjoys her food as you do, Ella.'

I glanced at Jacob. He was looking at me with a decided twinkle in those black eyes of his.

'Just making up for lost time,' I answered, at the same time idly glancing at the old grandfather clock standing in one corner of the room.

'Goodness! It's nearly eleven'

I was amazed. We had sat eating and drinking and talking for nearly four hours. Four hours that had passed in a flash.

'Well, Jacob, I have really enjoyed this evening. The food was delicious.'

'And I hope you enjoyed the company as much as I did.'

'That was also very pleasant. But I'm going to say goodnight before I become a rude guest and start nodding off at the table.'

Jacob rose and helped me with my chair. He escorted me to the bottom of the staircase, gave a quaint bow then bade me goodnight.

After having a quick peep at Matilda, who was sleeping soundly, I slowly undressed ready for bed.

Jacob had been the perfect host.

My first impression of an arrogant, aloof man who had no time for a couple of females from England had undergone a complete reversal.

He was very interesting to listen to, and had the rare knack of making one feel there was no one he would rather be spending time with.

If truth were told, being saddled with Matilda and I was probably the last thing he wanted, but not once did he give that impression.

Yes, I was favourably impressed with the commissioner.

My last memory of that lovely evening was being serenaded by the crickets, then oblivion.

BUSHVELD.

I woke to the screeching of peacocks.

Lying in bed, hands behind my head, I let my thoughts wander back to the past evening.

Thinking on what we'd talked about, I realised Jacob had deliberately kept the conversation away from the mine and all the happenings of the last few days.

Instead, he'd regaled me with humorous tales of events that had happened on the farm, as well as giving me an insight into his family.

His mother, Emily, had been living with her elder daughter Sylvia for the past year, since Jacob's father had died in an accident. Jacob hadn't elaborated on what had happened. Sylvia lived with her husband Tony and two children on a tobacco farm in the Triangle district. Emily had visited Tevrede a few times since her husband's death, but found the memories too much at the moment to contend with.

Jacob had another sister, Norma, who was unmarried, and living in Harare. She taught at an all girls' school.

Then there was Robert, the younger brother, who helped out on the farm, until he was able to resume his veterinarian studies in Onderstepoort, South Africa. When his father died, he put his training on hold to help Jacob, until a replacement for the commissioner's job became available. This had taken much longer than expected, but Jacob was hopeful it would come to fruition within the next week or so. Then he would be running the farm full time, and Robert could return to S.A.

Robert wasn't at dinner last night, as he was called out to help with a difficult calving.

'The local vet knows he's got a willing helper in my brother. I've never known anyone with such a love for animals.'

I told Jacob about the wire noose I'd seen in the bush with the duiker trapped in it.

'They're a scourge. Every time I come across one, I destroy it. My thoughts about these traps are very well known. I haven't seen any on Tevrede for a long time.'

And that's the way the conversation went. Easy, no awkward pauses at all.

There was a knock on my bedroom door. It opened, and Matilda's face appeared.

'Good, you're awake, I see,' and she padded into the bedroom and plonked herself down on my bed.

'Well, how did it go? Did you enjoy yourself last night?'

'I'm very pleased to see you looking so chipper, aunt, and yes, I had a lovely time. The food was delicious, the conversation scintillating, and the company very acceptable,' and I grinned at her.

'I can see a good night's sleep has done you the world of good. How's the headache?'

'Gone, I'm thankful to say. After the tea and soup, I was dead to the world until I heard screeching outside my window. I've been woken by crowing poultry before, but never by peacocks. I had no idea they made so much noise.'

'Just be thankful they don't wake up at the crack of dawn. What time is it, anyway?'

'Eight, and the weather is beautiful.'

She settled herself more comfortably on the bed.

'Did you and the commissioner mention our escapade by any chance?'

'No, we didn't actually. I was just thinking about how Jacob deliberately kept the conversation away from that nightmare, which was very thoughtful of him. We talked about our families and a host of other things.'

I pulled a face.

'I suppose we'll have to face up to the unpleasant aspect of our stay in Zimbabwe.'

'Well, no more detective work for us, Ella. We must leave everything to the authorities.'

She paused, and then continued talking.

'However, I've been thinking about that skeleton in the mine. You're going to think I'm going gaga even suggesting this, but could it possibly be Arthur Westbury's remains, or am I letting my imagination get the better of me?' and Matilda's voice trailed away as memories of our gruesome discovery came flooding back.

'You could be right. Quite a long shot though…Anyway, let's not think about that for now. I'm going to have a quick shower, and then we'll go down for breakfast. I'll meet you in your room in fifteen minutes,' and I jumped out of bed and gave Matilda a quick hug.

Twenty minutes later we were in the dining room enjoying flapjacks covered in syrup. This was after eating a bowl of mealie meal porridge coated in sugar and thick clotted cream. Freshly ground coffee wafted delicious aromas from our coffee cups, and I could see from the way Matilda tucked into her food, she was rapidly gaining her usual optimistic outlook on life.

The dining room door opened, and in strode the commissioner, dressed now in khaki shirt and shorts, bush hat in his hand.

'Good morning ladies. You both look well. How's your headache, Mrs. Syndham?'

'Gone, commissioner, and please call me Matilda. Thank you so much for your thoughtfulness last night with the tea and soup. I was telling Ella earlier, I was dead to the world until I heard the peacocks. A good night's sleep is often the best cure,' and Matilda sat there smiling happily at Jacob.

He turned to me.

'Thank you again for your company last night, Ella. I've arranged for my assistant to take charge of the office today as I thought you would enjoy a conducted tour of the farm. We could take a picnic lunch and have it at the dam. You're more than welcome to come Matilda, if you feel up to it.'

Aunt waved a hand in the air.

'No, I don't think so, Jacob. I shall be quite content selecting a book from your interesting library if that's ok with you. After the excitement of the last few days, a nice quiet day reading appeals to me.'

The commissioner smiled his understanding and then turned to face me.

'Well Ella, would you like a tour of the farm, or would you prefer resting at the farmhouse?'

'A tour of the farm sounds delightful. I would love it. What time did you want to leave?'

'Good. Meet me at the front of the house in twenty minutes. I'll have the jeep waiting. Make sure you bring a hat.'

And with that parting shot, he was out the door calling for Gloria to have a pack lunch ready by nine thirty.

'Well, you and the commissioner seem to be getting along well.'

'Are you sure you want to stay behind aunt?'

'Positive! I shall enjoy reading in the garden. I see the police guard is still in place, so, I shall be quite safe. You go and have a good time,' and she chuckled as she wiped her lips with her napkin. She then pushed her chair back and told me to hurry and get changed. I couldn't go bushwhacking in that dress, however much it may suit me.

A quick glance at the grandfather clock told me I had fifteen minutes.

I rushed up stairs and found jeans, t-shirt and my walking boots. A hat was a problem as mine was still at the bottom of the mineshaft.

'I'll find one for you,' said Jacob, after I told him of my predicament, and within a minute he was back holding a wide brim straw hat.

'It belongs to my mother. She won't mind you using it.'

We climbed into the jeep, and after making sure the picnic basket was safe, were soon bowling along the dirt road, Matilda waving us goodbye.

I settled in my seat, ready to enjoy myself.

Looking around, I noticed Jacob had a rifle tucked next to him.

'Do you always take a gun with you when you drive on the farm?'

'Always. These are wild animals we have here. And although they look peaceful from a distance, if you're walking through the bush and you come across a buck or baboon, or even a leopard, you have to be prepared to shoot if it's obvious it's going to attack. It doesn't happen often, of course, because they sense us long before we have an inkling of their presence. However, mothers with babies are especially dangerous; but obviously, we take as much care as possible not to disturb them.'

We drove on the main dirt road for about fifteen minutes, and then took a left turn. The mealie fields were soon left behind, and we were plunging into the indigenous African bush.

Jacob parked the jeep and we began walking. It all looked very similar to what Matilda and I had seen these last couple of days, but with one big difference. I was with someone who had grown up in this environment.

Jacob knew every bush, tree and plant by name. He pointed out plants the different African tribes used for medicinal purposes, which ones were good for the pot, and those to avoid at all costs as they were poisonous. He showed me the spoor of different animals, even the variations between male and female buck. To be honest, I couldn't tell the difference, but to Jacob, it was as easy as telling black from white.

Whilst walking in single file, following an animal track, I spotted a bush a little way ahead, covered in white berries.

'Those look interesting. What are they?'

'They're called voelent. When the berries are chewed, they become sticky, like chewing gum. The Africans chew them, and then stick them on bushes near a favourite watering hole for birds. The birds get stuck, so they are easy to catch'.

Further along, I was amazed to see a huge number of bright yellow birds darting around and asked Jacob about them.

'Weaverbirds, so called because they weave intricate nests. They tend to favour one tree, and all build their nests in that tree. If you look over there you can see hundreds of hanging nests. At times they become pests when their numbers suddenly multiply. I've seen swarms of them two kilometres wide and one kilometre deep. They can decimate a farmer's maize crop in a day'

We made a detour back to the jeep and Jacob drove us down the track onto the dirt road, which we followed through the fields again. We drove between hills, gradually climbing all the time. Jacob stopped the jeep on the brow of a hill, and untied the picnic basket.

'The dam is just over that kopje and it's nearly one; definitely time for lunch. Are you hungry?'

'I thought after such a huge breakfast, I wouldn't be hungry for hours, but with the amount of walking we've done, I'm ravenous.'

'Good. Just bring the blanket Gloria put behind your seat and follow me.'

Jacob strode ahead with the basket, and disappeared behind some rocks. I grabbed the blanket and hurried after him.

The view that greeted me was astonishing.

Stretching below was the dam, the aquamarine water mirroring the cloudless sky, shimmering like multitudes of sapphires in the sunlight. It was nestled in a valley, deeply sloping sides covered in typical African bush, the colours of green and gold foliage making a superb backdrop.

Standing there, it seemed as though Jacob and I were the only people on earth.

The commissioner took the blanket and spread it on a flat rock.

'This is lovely,' and I leant back against a rock that had a natural curve, my back fitting perfectly.

'I could sit here for hours just looking and listening. It's so peaceful. How you must love it.'

'You're right. I do love it. It's my favourite part of the farm. Very few people know it exists. In fact, I've never shared it with anyone outside the family before'

There was a pause.

'But down to business. Let's see what Gloria packed in the basket,' and he lifted the lid and unpacked our picnic lunch.

I helped lay out knives, forks and plates on a tablecloth, whilst mentally giving myself a shake. 'Don't read too much into what Jacob says,' I admonished myself. 'He's just being friendly, that's all, and anyway, you're not interested.'

The lunch was delicious. Cold meat and salads followed by watermelon, washed down with a bottle of ice-cold wine from the Tevrede cellar.

I sat back against my rock.

The wine made me drowsy, and with the background noises of birds and insects sounding like a lullaby, I could feel my eyelids getting heavy.

I awoke with my cheek being stroked.

'Oh, I'm so sorry! I didn't mean to nod off like that.'

'You looked so peaceful I didn't have the heart to disturb you, but unfortunately, it's time we were getting back to the farm.'

The sun had settled lower in the sky. I'd been sleeping for over an hour.

'I think these last few days have been more of a strain than I realised, or maybe I ought to blame your wine. I'm not normally such bad company.'

'I'll bring you back at sunset sometime, and then you'll see a host of animals come to the dam to drink. This is a favourite watering hole for many different types of buck, including kudu. Wildebeest and warthog also make use of it. We had elephant and lion, but with so much land being used for crops and grazing, they had to be resettled on game reserves or areas not used for farming. I also remember seeing giraffe here as a child.'

I scrambled off the blanket and folded it. Jacob held out his hand to help me over the rocks and didn't let go until we were back at the jeep. With the basket safely stowed, we climbed in and drove back to the main dirt road leading to the farmhouse.

I was wishing the day could continue forever, but, as the saying goes, all good things come to an end, and how true that turned out to be.

Turning left into the driveway, I saw a strange car parked at the end of the drive, and who should be standing by it, but Aunt Matilda and the unmistakable figure of Inspector Stuart.

BACK TO REALITY.

I couldn't believe it. Being jerked back to reality after such an unforgettable day was awful.

I looked at Jacob, stunned!

'Why on earth is Inspector Stuart here?'

'Well,' said the commissioner, 'Sergeant Ndlovu obviously had to inform the UK authorities about your adventures, for want of a better word, and was put in contact with Inspector Stuart, who said he would arrive as soon as possible. I deliberately didn't say anything as I was hoping that meant tomorrow, but at least you had one day without worrying about murders and such like.'

By this time we'd stopped behind the inspector's car.

Matilda came bustling over saying, 'Look whose here, Ella. It's our inspector. How wonderful he came so quickly…and the most amazing coincidence…Jacob and the inspector know each other!'

Before I could react to that bit of astonishing news, the inspector turned to me and said, 'Ah, Dr Stanbridge. Your aunt was telling me how you saved her from almost certain death. You seem to be a very enterprising young woman. However, as I explained to Mrs. Syndham, no more amateur sleuthing please. Leave it to the professionals. You might not be so fortunate next time.'

'That's exactly what I said to Ella this morning, inspector. No more detective work for us, and we do apologise for any problems we've given you, don't we Ella?'

I just nodded.

The inspector then held his hand out to Jacob.

'Good to see you again, commissioner, although I wish under different circumstances.'

Jacob shook the proffered hand and agreed with the inspector's sentiments.

Anyway, let's go inside. We could all do with a drink, I'm sure,' and the commissioner led the way.

I followed everyone up the steps into the house.

'Ella, I'm sure you want to freshen up a little. Let's leave the men to chinwag for a while. Is that alright with you commissioner?'

And before Jacob could answer, Matilda grabbed my arm and was whisking me up the stairs at a rate of knots.

I looked back at Jacob, who gave a rueful grin before following Inspector Stuart into the library.

'What on earth is going on aunt? What's the hurry?' and tried prising my arm loose from Matilda's pincer like grip.

'Shhh, let's wait until we reach my room.'

I glanced at her and was surprised to see how apprehensive she looked.

Once her bedroom door was closed, she reached out and hugged me so hard I was forced to protest.

'Aunt! What is wrong with you? Did anything happen today I should know about?'

'Goodness, I've been so worried. I was absolutely petrified an accident was going to happen to you and I wouldn't be there to prevent it. And he seems such a nice man.'

I stared at her, totally bewildered.

'What man are you talking about? Jacob?'

'Shhh, not so loud. He might hear us.'

Now I was worried. Had being trapped down the mine affected my poor aunt more than I realised?

She read my thoughts.

'No, I'm not going mad, Ella. At least, I don't think so. Go and sit on my bed.'

I dutifully sat and waited for an explanation.

'Have you shown the commissioner the two scarves?'

'No I haven't. Anyway, we decided not to tell him about the scarves, fax or the printout, remember? Why do you ask?'

'Because of this,' and Matilda opened a drawer in her bedside cabinet and pulled out a scarf that looked similar to the two I had, or thought I had.

'Where did you find it? I thought I'd tucked them safely away in my room'

'This isn't one of those scarves, Ella. This is another one.'

'Another one! How can that be?'

'I found it in Jacob's library.'

'In Jacob's library?' I know. I sound like an echo.

She nodded.

'This whole scenario just gets more weird and convoluted! And then to have Inspector Stuart arrive like that!'

'Okay. Just tell me from the beginning how all this came about.'

Matilda sat next to me on the bed and took one of my hands in hers.

'After I waved goodbye this morning, I went into the library to find a book to read. I must say the commissioner has a wide range of books to choose from.'

'Stick to the story!'

'Sorry. Well, I was picking out a book here and a book there, not able to choose one I really wanted when I saw an old thick one titled, 'Exploring Zimbabwe. A detailed study of the Midlands Area,' and took it off the bookshelf. As I did so, I noticed a tiny piece of silk hanging from inside the spine of the book. I pulled and was left holding this scarf! Once I got over the shock of finding it; I hid the scarf away, and have been pacing the floor ever since, willing for you to appear. And then Inspector Stuart arrives out of the blue a few minutes before you. What a relief to see Jacob's jeep pull up behind his car with you in it. I have been imagining the worse, I can tell you.'

I stared at Matilda, trying to make sense of this latest development.

Why was a third scarf hidden in a book on Zimbabwe? How did Jacob get hold of the scarf in the first place? Was his being friendly to me, only a means to gain my trust and confidence?

'None of this is making any sense. There must be some sort of logical explanation, aunt. There must be'

Aunt looked at me doubtfully

'I'm sure there is, Ella.'

I rose from the bed.

'I haven't a clue as to what to think... Listen, aunt. I'm going to get changed for dinner. We'll discuss it later. Don't worry. We'll find out what's going on'

Standing under the shower, the hot water slowly dissolved the numb feeling enveloping me. I was furious with myself. Jacob was using me for his own purposes. Well, two can play at that game, and after dressing and taking extra care with makeup and hair, I marched into Matilda's room, ready to do battle.

Aunt looked at me with misgiving.

'Are you feeling all right, Ella? I'm not sure if I trust that glint in your eye.'

'I'm fine aunt, but I think we agree Jacob must be up to something, and we're going to find out what it is. Come on; let's go to dinner. Gloria's banging the gong. Who knows what information we may get at the dining room table? Maybe Jacob will let something slip.'

I ushered Matilda out of the bedroom door and we hurried down the stairs to join Jacob and Inspector Stuart coming out of the library. The look in Jacob's eyes told me the extra care I'd taken was appreciated. He offered me his arm to escort me into the dining room, whilst Inspector Stuart did the same with Matilda.

I glanced at Jacob as he pulled out my chair. He gave me a warm smile. I smiled back. Matilda was chatting away to the inspector.

Gloria's cooking was true to form, absolutely delicious, but I was in no mood to appreciate it. My mind was on other things as in between the small talk, I attempted to unravel in my mind the tangled web Matilda and I had become involved in. Several times I noticed Jacob looking at me with an intensity I would have found flattering an hour or so ago. But circumstances had changed drastically since our picnic at the dam.

When it was time for coffee, Inspector Stuart asked us to go through our ordeal step by step.

'I'll record what you say then get it typed up and you can sign it.'

'That'll be fine, inspector. Our assailant admitted killing Philip and Mr. Short didn't he aunt?'

She nodded as I continued; 'They must be caught before they murder anyone else.'

I told the inspector everything that had happened since arriving in Zimbabwe, but kept quiet about the scarves. Obviously, the inspector wanted to know why we were at the mine. Aunt chipped in about recognising the name Makokoshla and what an adventure it would be if we could find the mine, never dreaming we would be attacked in such a horrible way.

'And that brings you up to date, inspector.'

'Good. That gives me an excellent start in catching them. That's enough for tonight, Dr Stanbridge…Dr Stanbridge?'

I came to with a jerk, to find three pairs of eyes looking at me.

'I'm so sorry, inspector, and please call me Ella. My mind wandered for a moment.'

Little did he know I'd had a brainwave regarding the scarves! I couldn't wait to get back up stairs. I looked at the grandfather clock. Nine p.m.

'I hope you don't mind, but I'm for an early night. All that fresh air has made me really tired.'

'And I'll join you, Ella,' said Matilda pushing back her chair.

A look of disappointment crossed Jacob's face but he only said,' Sleep well. I really enjoyed today. Remember what I said about showing you the dam at sunset.'

'I'm looking forward to it. Goodnight inspector,' and made a quick exit out of the dining room, leaving Matilda to hurriedly say her goodnights.

She followed me up the staircase.

'You are on to something, Ella. I can sense it.'

I grinned at her before opening her bedroom door. Once inside, I sat on the bed and said, 'Did you notice the large standard lamp in the dining room, aunt?'

'The brass lamp near that beautiful grandfather clock?'

'That's the one.'

'What of it?'

'Did you notice the lampshade? It's made out of a silky material.'

'So?'

'Did you see the way the light shone through the material illuminating the pattern on the fabric?'

Understanding dawned.

She switched on the bedside lamp whilst I went next door to get the other two scarves. I placed them on top of each other. We held them up to the light and studied the resultant pattern carefully.

Nothing.

I changed the combination.

Still nothing.

'Third time lucky,' said Matilda, and she was right.

There, as plain as day, was the word TEVREDE showing through the top right hand corner. I could make out the farmhouse and the main dirt road running through the farmlands. It was amazing! Just like looking at a three- dimensional picture. There was no mistaking what we were seeing; a detailed study of the farm and surrounding area. The only problem was the scarves were so large, we could only see a small piece at a time, which was very frustrating.

'Whoever did this was brilliant,' said Matilda. 'Silk screening three scarves separately instead of one scarf three times. This reminds me of the 3D films that were popular in the fifties at the cinema. I remember wearing special spectacles to get this optical illusion effect. It was mesmerizing.'

'We need to find a way to see the whole thing in one go, and I believe I know how to do it, but we'll have to wait for morning. These bedrooms face east. The sun shines through early, so if we stick the scarves onto the window, the light from the sun will illuminate them, the same as the bedside lamp, and we shall see the whole picture.'

'That's a great idea, Ella. At last the mystery of the scarves will be solved,' and Matilda gave a little jig around the bed.

'I wonder where this will lead. Will it give us a clue to the connection between Tevrede and Makokoshla mine?'

'Aunt! Do you think Jacob will miss the scarf?'

'The book was dusty when I took it off the bookshelf. We don't even know if he knew it was there. It was pure luck my noticing it. And I didn't open it to read, so it doesn't look as though it's been touched. No, I'm sure we're quite safe in having it tonight. We'll copy the picture on paper tomorrow morning. Then, to be on the safe side, I'll return the scarf back to its hiding place in the book.'

'Right then aunt. I'm going to say goodnight and I'll see you early in the morning,' and after putting the scarves away, I gave Matilda a hug and went to my room, only to dream of Jacob pointing his finger at me saying, 'I fooled you,' over and over and over again.

EUREKA.

The next morning on waking, the events of the evening flooded my brain, and I remembered the disillusionment I felt when realising Jacob was not the person I thought he was, although was I jumping to conclusions?

'Doesn't matter one way or the other. It's not important,' I said aloud, and padded in bare feet to the window to check the weather.

'Good. The sun's shining and not a cloud in the sky. Another ten minutes and it will shine directly into Matilda's bedroom.'

I quickly washed and dressed and then went next door to aunt's room.

After tapping softly, I walked in to find her still in the land of nod.

'Wake up, aunt,' and gently shook her shoulder.

'But the peacock hasn't started his infernal racket yet,' she grumbled, sitting up in bed. 'What time is it?'

'Six thirty and the sun will be shining through your window very soon. We haven't a minute to lose. I don't want anyone seeing what we're doing from outside the house.'

I left Matilda to her grumbling, and took the scarves out of the drawer.

'Where's the sticky tape?'

'In my carpet bag.'

Once found, I arranged the scarves in the right order and stuck a piece of tape over each corner.

'Are you ready, aunt? I'm going to need help in sticking them on the window.'

She came out of the bathroom, and took hold of two sides whilst I had the other two. We carried the scarves to the window, and laid them on the carpet. I drew back the curtains to be rewarded with a beam of sun shining on my face.

'Perfect,' and after making sure no one was lurking outside, we lifted the scarves into position, and pressed the tape to secure them.

We stood back to get a better view.

'Amazing,' said Matilda, and with sketch pad and pencil in hand began drawing the picture that was now so apparent.

I studied it carefully.

It was definitely a picture, not a map. The farmhouse was central with the dirt road easily seen, skirting the hills and valleys, the dam nestling in between the hills at the top left hand corner.

I looked closer.

'A replica of the fig tree at Makokoshla mine is in the bottom left hand corner. Look aunt. No mistaking that tree.'

'I'm sketching it now. What is that between the branches? Can you see?'

'Not without your magnifying glass,' and I retrieved the glass from Matilda's bag.

'Numbers and letters are disguised amongst the branches of the tree. This is so clever. I'll read them out.'

Within fifteen minutes, aunt had a drawing done with all relevant landmarks pencilled in.

'Let's take it down before anyone sees it,' and we pulled the tapes loose from the window, just as the last beam of sunlight moved away.

'Just in time,' and I glanced at Matilda's clock.

Seven o'clock.

After folding the scarves and putting them back in the drawer, we sat on the bed and studied Matilda's handiwork.

'Can you remember which scarf you took out of the book, aunt? We don't want to put the wrong one back.'

'I know which one it is. It has a dark spot in the middle.'

'Good. Now then, those numbers and letters you copied are, hopefully, coordinates. We haven't used the fax yet. Maybe those two will tie up, as we used the printout to find the mine. Now, I need the Jetta's keys.'

'Why?'

'To go back to the mine of course. I know we won't get so close to it as we did with the land rover, but I don't think we should risk trying to hire another one. A little bit further to walk won't be a problem will it?'

'No, of course not. But do you think this is a wise move?'

'Absolutely. We aren't prisoners here, for heaven's sake. How else are we going to find out what is going on?'

Matilda shrugged and said,' Fine. No need to get shirty!'

I gave her a hug and apologised.

She hugged me back, gave a knowing look and said, 'I understand.'

Making sure we hadn't left any evidence of the last half hours activities, we walked into the dining room to find both Jacob and Inspector Stuart tucking into eggs and bacon.

'Good morning Ella, Matilda. Slept well, I hope,' said Jacob, and he rose to help me with my chair.

'Gloria will bring your breakfast now. Unfortunately, I'm needed at the office, but I'll try and get away early.'

'That's sweet of you, Jacob. By the way, where do you keep the Jetta keys?'

'In a drawer in the library. Why? You're not thinking of going anywhere are you?

I smiled, shook my head and concentrated on eating the bowl of porridge Gloria had put in front of me.

'Well, ladies, 'said the inspector. 'I'm going to the mine this morning. We need to see if we can identify the skeleton you spoke about. You seem to think it could be Arthur Westbury, Mrs Syndham?'

'Well, I can't be certain, of course, but things do tend to point that way.'

'I'll need the coordinates for the mine, Ella.'

'No problem, inspector,' but alarm bells were ringing in my head.

How could we go back to the mine without arousing the inspector's suspicions?

Then, of course, the obvious answer came to me.

'You know, inspector, I could show you where the mine is. Why don't I go with you?'

'Are you sure you want to re-visit the place where you had such a terrible ordeal?'

'That won't bother me. What do you say, aunt? Shall we go with the inspector?'

'Absolutely.'

'Right. That will be a great help. I need to phone Sergeant Ndlovu while you finish your breakfast. I'll meet you at the front of the house in twenty minutes.'

'I'll hold you responsible, Charles, if anything happens to Ella or her aunt,' Jacob warned the inspector.

'Don't worry about them, Jacob. They'll be safe as houses with me.'

Jacob said his goodbyes, and we heard him roar off in his jeep.

Matilda and I finished our breakfast and went back to aunt's bedroom. I was eager to compare the figures in the fig tree with the fax. Aunt wanted to put the scarf back, but she had a problem as Inspector Stuart was using the phone in the library.

'Don't worry aunt. He won't be there for long.'

I smoothed the fax out on the bed and poured over the figures to find comparisons, and again, the relevant ones stood out like a sore thumb. I took out the map and traced the coordinates.

Something interesting showed up.

The place I marked on the map was a little distance from the mine. If my estimation was correct, the place marked was at the outcrop of rock where we'd drank the water and admired the view.

'I wonder what's so interesting about those rocks that's worth killing for,' said Matilda.

'Philip and Mr Short were obviously figuring out the puzzle before they were killed. What was the company called again that gave you the scarf?'

'Swingen Linen. Remember I said it was a present for work done on the Queen of Sheba theme. I've a feeling someone made a huge mistake, and gave me the wrong scarf!'

'Whom did you deal with at the company?'

'A rather self-opinionated woman calling herself Stephanie Stone. I'll never forget her. She had a lot of very frizzy dyed blond hair, and an extremely long chin. She reminded me of Punch.'

'Punch?'

'Yes! Punch in the Punch and Judy puppet show.'

This Stephanie had not made a good impression on Aunt Matilda.

'Try and remember as much as you can about the time you worked for that company. Who knows, maybe those two goons are working for Stephanie Stone.'

'That's quite an accusation, Ella.'

'I'm just suspicious of everyone now we know Jacob has some personal involvement in all of this.'

Aunt Matilda shook her head. I could see she was still hoping some reasonable explanation would crop up exonerating Jacob.

I wasn't feeling so charitable.

'When we get to the outcrop, you must say you're too tired to carry on. I'll point Inspector Stuart in the right direction to the mine, and then we'll have some time to look around the area. Who knows? We might come across something.'

By the time we'd organized ourselves, the inspector was coming out of the library.

'I'll bring the car to the front,' he called, and went out the door.

'Quick, aunt! Now's our chance to put the scarf back.'

We went into the library, and Matilda stuffed the scarf back in its original hiding place.

We were standing on the steps of the veranda when the blue sedan the inspector was driving, appeared round the corner of the house.

'Righto ladies. In you get.'

And we were off to Gweru police station, and then to the mine.

A VITAL FIND.

Gweru was a twenty minute drive from Tevrede.

The police station was built on colonial lines similar to many of the government buildings in this country; black corrugated roof, khaki coloured building surrounded by a green veranda was the order of the day.

Inspector Stuart hopped out of the sedan, walked briskly into the station, and within minutes, reappeared with four constables, a forensic expert carrying his bag of tricks, and an assortment of ropes, torches etc. draped over everyone's arms.

'Jump to it, men!' he barked, and they all scrambled into two of the three jeeps that had pulled up behind us.

'Ladies. If you don't mind getting out of the car, we shall be using this police vehicle. It's more suitable than the sedan. You did say the track was quite rough, eh?'

'We won't be able to park too close to the mine. There's a fair bit of walking involved,' said Matilda, and she clambered out of the car, clutching her carpetbag. She climbed into the back of the jeep whilst I sat in the front to give directions.

We were soon bowling along the dirt road towards the fork. Once reached, this was my cue to help the inspector. I led us to where we'd parked a few days previously.

'Now comes the hard bit,' and I began hiking up the steep track towards the outcrop of rocks. There was a fair bit of puffing and panting behind me, as the inspector did his best to keep up.

'Just as well you changed out of your pin striped suit, inspector. It wouldn't have lasted long on this hike'

'Jacob leant me a shirt and pair of shorts. I didn't have time to get anything appropriate before I left England, except a pair of walking boots I was able to bring.'

We plodded steadily upwards.

I'd forgotten how steep and long the walk had been. One of the policemen had gallantly offered to carry Matilda's bag, an offer I could see he was very much regretting.

'Is it much further?' and I looked behind to see Inspector Stuart, very red in the face, obviously hoping the answer would be no.

'The hard slog is over,' and I stepped into the opening.

'My word! This is absolutely magnificent,' he exclaimed.

'Yes. This view is worth the hike,' and I sat down on the same rock I'd used before.

Matilda came to join me.

'How are you doing, aunt?'

'I'm fine,' she said quietly.

She gave me a quick hug, and then informed the inspector she was going to stay at the outcrop whilst the rest of us went on to the mine.

'Feeling tired, aunt? I'll stay with you. Inspector, I'll point you in the right direction to get to the mine. You can't miss it, I promise. Do you want to rest longer or shall we get going?'

'I think one of the constables should stay behind with Mrs. Syndham,' replied the inspector.

'No, that won't be necessary,' said aunt. 'You need all the help available. Let Ella show you the track you need to take, and we'll wait here for your return. This view is so superb; I could sit here looking at it for hours.'

The inspector wasn't keen on leaving us. I could hear him muttering about what Jacob would say if he knew aunt and I would be left on our own.

'Come, inspector. Time is passing. Let me show you the way. The sooner you get to the mine, the sooner you'll finish what you have to do,' and before the inspector could protest anymore, I walked back into the bush.

Ten minutes on, I told Inspector Stuart to keep on the track the way we were going and it would lead him directly to the mine.

'I'd better get back to aunt. See you later.'

Matilda was sitting where I'd left her.

'I'm sure the inspector is suspicious,' I said, before clambering on a rock near her.

'Well, let's hope he keeps his suspicions under control until we find what we're looking for. Are you sure this is the place? I had a quick look round whilst you were gone and couldn't find anything.'

'I'm positive. Those co-ordinates in the fig tree definitely refer to this outcrop. I haven't a clue as to what we're looking for, but I'm positive it's here, whatever it is.'

'You look on that side,' said aunt, pointing with her right hand, 'and I'll take the left. Now, just be careful. That's a long drop down there'

We split up, and I slowly moved over the rocks on the right side of the outcrop.

'Watch out for snakes and scorpions. If you turn a rock over, use your foot.'

'Don't worry, aunt. I'll be careful.'

We searched for something, anything, for about thirty minutes. Nothing.

Stopping for a drink of water out of the container I'd carried with me, Matilda shook her head and said, 'This is discouraging, Ella. I thought we might have found something by now.'

'I know. However, we've one more place left to look.'

'Where? We've gone over this piece of ground inch by inch.'

'Below us.'

'You mean, below the overhang?'

'Yes. That could be an ideal place to hide something. I wish I'd thought of it earlier. It's out of the way of the elements and certainly not easily found, as we can vouch for. I'm going to climb down the rocks over there and make my way around to below where we are sitting now. It shouldn't be too difficult.'

Before Matilda could protest, I was up and gone.

Within five minutes, I was calling to aunt from about ten feet below her.

'Aunt! Can you see me?'

'No, although you sound very close.'

'Lie on your stomach and put your head over the edge.'

She did just that, and saw me grinning up at her.

'It's actually quite easy getting here, almost as though the way was hewn out of the rock. And guess what I've found.'

'What?'

'A cave.'

'Now we're getting somewhere. Does it look hopeful?'

'If I had a light I would be able to tell you.'

'Let me get my torch.'

Within minutes, Matilda was lying on her stomach, lowering the torch she'd tied to a piece of string she'd found in her carpetbag. I grabbed it as it swung close to my head and then disappeared into the cave.

It was small.

Several large rocks protected the entrance, but there was a narrow opening I was able to squeeze through. It wasn't visible from the outside unless you were right up close.

A very good hiding place.

Once inside, I swung the beam of light onto the walls. They were dry, and stretched back about fifteen feet from the entrance. I shone the torch from the left hand side of the cave, sweeping it from floor to ceiling, which was about eight foot high. I inched my way to the back of the cave, making sure I didn't miss any potential hiding places.

The problem was I had no idea what I was looking for; it could even be writing on the wall for all I knew. I was also concerned Inspector Stuart might make an appearance. I didn't want him to find me in the cave.

'Any luck, Ella?'

'Nothing at the moment,'

I moved closer to the back of the cave, peering into any likely hiding places, but hiding what and what size?

This was really trying to find the proverbial needle in the haystack.

Then, as I was getting more convinced I had totally misread everything, my search was rewarded.

Tucked away at the back of the cave, hidden behind rocks that had been carefully piled on top of one another, I found a leather saddlebag.

I was shaking with excitement as I pulled it out from its hiding place.

'Aunt! Are you there? I've found something!'

'What is it?'

'A saddle bag with initials stamped on it.'

'What are they?'

'An A and a W.'

'Surely that could only be Arthur Westbury!'

It didn't take long to climb back around the overhang and onto the rocky plateau where Matilda was waiting for me. She helped me up the last few feet, and I handed her the saddlebag. She ran her fingers over the initials, obviously feeling emotional over the memories they were bringing to mind.

'Poor, poor Arthur.'

'Aunt! Can you hear voices? I bet that's the inspector coming back from the mine. Quick! Let's put the saddlebag inside yours.'

And not a minute too soon.

'Ah, ladies! I hope we didn't keep you waiting too long. We found the skeleton as you described, and the forensic chappie did his thing. It must have been extremely unpleasant for you down there. Even with all our lights and equipment, I was glad to get to the surface. Do you feel fit enough to walk back to the vehicles, Mrs. Syndham?'

'Absolutely, inspector. The rest has really refreshed me. There's nothing like looking at a beautiful view for a while to become rested physically and mentally.

'Good, good.'

The inspector turned to one of his constables.

'Just carry Mrs Syndham's bag for her, although why you feel it necessary to lug such a large bag around with you all the time, I really don't know.'

'Put it down to an old lady's foibles,' she said grinning. 'I would be lost without it.'

We all trooped back down the track to where the vehicles were parked.

I couldn't wait to get back to the house to see what was inside the saddlebag. Were we finally solving the mystery, or was it going to be another step in unravelling the puzzle? I could see Matilda was just as impatient.

Going down the track was obviously much easier than the trek up, so we reached the jeeps in half the time it took us to go the other way.

Arriving at the police station, we all disembarked, Inspector Stuart disappearing with the other members of the force, whilst we waited for him in the sedan.

'I wish he'd hurry up,' said Matilda. 'The suspense is killing me! I'm sure Arthur hid the saddlebag before he was killed. To think this whole saga goes back all those years.'

'The inspector's coming, aunt.'

'Sorry to keep you waiting. I'll drop you off at the farm, and then I'll come back. I've a lot of work to do on this case. It's becoming quite complicated. Who would have guessed, Mrs. Syndham, finding Philip Westbury dead in your lounge would have led to a gold mine in Africa.'

'It really is amazing how things turn out, inspector,' said Matilda. 'But I'm sure once you've found our assailants, all will be explained.'

We swept up the drive, and the inspector stopped by the steps leading up to the farm house.

CLARIFICATION.

We stood and patiently waved the inspector goodbye.

Then, like two bullets out of a gun, shot through the front door, and raced upstairs.

I placed the carpet bag on aunt's bed and removed the saddlebag.

'Go on, aunt. You do the honours. After all, Arthur Westbury was your acquaintance.'

Matilda undid the buckles on one side and pulled out a bundle of papers tied with string, which she laid on the bed. She unbuckled the other side and retrieved a weathered parchment of skin folded in quarters.

Unfolding the skin, aunt exclaimed in surprise, 'another map!'

'Let me see,' and I leant over her shoulder to get a better look. Sure enough, someone had burnt a map on the parchment of skin.

'I'll study it just now. Let's see what's in the bundle of papers,' and untied the string and gave the packet to aunt.

Matilda became engrossed in what she was reading. The paper she held looked official. I waited patiently until she'd finished.

She raised her head, a bewildered expression on her face.

'Well. What does it say?'

'It's title deeds to a property. And if I'm not mistaken, the property is Tevrede.'

That didn't make any sense. But then, what part of this whole saga did?

'Why would Arthur Westbury be carrying title deeds to this farm?'

'It's not just the farm. The mining rights are mentioned as well.'

'Whose name is on the deeds?'

'Jacob Muller.'

'That would be right. Jacob told me this farm has been in his family for generations.'

'There's more,' said Matilda. 'Attached to the deeds is a note, like an IOU. It's signed by Jacob Muller stating Arthur Westbury won the farm fair and square in a poker game'

'What!'

I couldn't believe what I was hearing. A huge farm lost and won on the turn of a playing card.

'No aunt. There must be some mistake. Who would be so foolish as to stake their livelihood on a poker game?'

'I'm not mistaken, Ella. See for yourself,' and Matilda handed me the deeds with the IOU attached.

She was right. There was no mistaking the intention of the note. Arthur Westbury had won this farm in a poker game.

'No wonder he was murdered. The Muller family must've been beside themselves when they found out the farm had been lost, especially in a card game. Can you believe that? But Arthur hid the saddlebag before he was murdered and the deeds and the IOU note could be destroyed. This secret has been kept all these years until Philip Westbury, relative so many times removed, must have heard about it and was trying to find proof of ownership of Tevrede.'

I paced the bedroom, trying to put together the pieces of the puzzle we had.

'Aunt, I'm going to write down what we know so far. There's so many different parts and people involved, I'm losing track,' and I took her sketching pad and pencil and made notes.

'Let's start with Arthur Westbury,' and I draw a column with his name.

'Okay. He won Tevrede, and was probably murdered because of his winning streak at poker. Body or rather, skeleton found in Makokoshla mine. Philip Westbury is next. Arthur Westbury was his, what… grandfather? Philip somehow found out about Tevrede and was murdered. Frederick Short, Philip's uncle, who was an art dealer, was helping Philip stake his claim, and was murdered as well.

I paused for a moment before saying aloud what had been running through my mind.

'Would Jacob Muller commit murder to hang on to his inheritance?'

'Oh I really hope not, Ella. He seems such a nice young man'

'Well, whether we like it or not, it is a possibility. Now, what else do we have? Our two assailants. Did Jacob Muller employ them as his hit men, but if so, why didn't he finish us off when he saw they had failed or does he think it too risky at this time. Does he want the dust to settle so to speak? And where do Stephanie and Swingen Linen come into the equation? Let's make another column for them.

You worked for the company a year ago and had a scarf given you as a thank you present. Let's make a separate column for the scarves, one given to you, one found in Frederick Short's office and one found in Jacob's library. Put together, they make one whole.

Now, what else do we have?

The mine… place where Arthur was murdered, or was his body dumped there, the murder taking place somewhere else? Right. Now the fig tree. Featured prominently on the scarves because of the co-ordinates hidden in the branches, also mentioned in Arthur's letters.'

I studied the lists carefully.

'You know, I can tie up everything except Swingen Linen.'

'Don't forget Swingen Linen was in Frederick Short's address book,' observed Matilda.

'True. I suppose that's a connection of sorts. Something we must follow up. Right, so the question is, did the Muller family have anything to do with the deaths of Arthur, Philip and Frederick?'

'I can't help thinking there's more to it than that, Ella. To murder Arthur, I suppose I can picture the rage and anger that did that. But the other two? Surely after all this time, the farm wouldn't have belonged to them. There must be a loophole or is it called statute of limitations, which would've prevented Philip from claiming the winnings. No one had to resort to murder unless much more was at stake.'

Matilda had a point.

But what was it that was so valuable murder was risked, including trying to finish off aunt and myself?

'Let's look at the map on the skin. Maybe that will give us some idea,' and I spread the hide out on the bed.

We studied it carefully.

It was crudely done. The ubiquitous fig tree featured prominently. What was interesting though, were the lines that were burnt, some zigzagging across each other, some ending on any part of the map, except one line appearing more prominent than the others. It was boldly burnt, and had a definite beginning and end. There were compass points marked on the line where it made detours.

'I wonder what these lines signify.'

'Well, the fig tree appears in the middle of them, so we must be looking at something connected to the mine.'

'Then these lines could be passages in the mine itself? The important one is obviously the one with the compass point directions. It's pointing in the direction of Tevrede.'

'Do you think so, Ella? We took quite a while to drive from the farm to the mine.'

'Actually, Tevrede is close to the mine if you go straight through the hillside. Don't forget, we had to drive around the hills to get here.'

'So, although it pains me to say so, there's more to find in that mine.'

'And only one way to find out what it is.'

Matilda looked at me, a frown on her face.

'That would not be a good idea.'

'No aunt. I'm not suggesting we go back to the mineshaft as such. What I am saying, is, we must try and find the entrance to the mine on Tevrede. Look where the bold line starts, somewhere near the farmhouse, because that square down there,' and I pointed to the bottom left hand corner of the map,' that square is the farmhouse, I'm sure.'

'You could be right. There is a T written in the centre.'

'What time is it, aunt? Goodness, nearly five. Too late to start looking now. We'll have to wait 'til morning, straight after breakfast. I hope Jacob has to go to the office again.'

'I still can't believe that nice young man had anything to do with the murders, Ella. I'm convinced there's an explanation for the scarf found in the library. Maybe I over reacted when I found it. The more I see Jacob, the more convinced I am he's not a murderer. He is far too nice to be one.'

'And what does a murderer look like? They don't exactly advertise themselves for what they really are. There's something else puzzling me. You said Inspector Stuart and Jacob know each other. Have you any idea how that came about?'

'No. The inspector just said it's a while since I've seen the commissioner, and then you both drove up in the land rover.'

Matilda must have realised there was no reasoning with me on that subject of Jacob because she abruptly changed direction.

'Let's shower and put our glad rags on for dinner. I'm sure Inspector Stuart will have a lot to talk about regarding the day's events, although we must hide the saddlebag away somewhere,' and looked vaguely around her room.

'I'll keep it in my room,' and I put everything back in the pouches and went next door to change.

Dinner was a lively affair.

Jacob's brother Robert joined us for the first time since we'd arrived at the farm. He was interested in hearing about everything, so the conversation never flagged. He kept voicing wild theories of why all this had happened.

As I sat listening to him, I couldn't help thinking how he would react if told of Jacob's potential involvement. Would he still regard his brother with the same loyalty and respect he obviously felt? How this family would be torn apart if the facts that seemed so incriminating came to light.

'You look sad, Ella. What's troubling you?'

Jacob's hand touched my arm, his magnetic eyes looking steadily into mine with such warmth, my own filled with tears.

I quickly blinked them away and smiled brightly at him.

'No Jacob, I'm fine. Are you going to the office tomorrow, or have you the day off?'

He held my gaze for a moment, and then answered, 'my new replacement is coming tomorrow to have a look around, so of course I must be there. Once he's settled in, we'll be able to spend another day together.

I'm looking forward to it very much. There's so much I want to show you.'

'So am I,' I said readily, and then continued eating my meal.

It was good news Jacob was going to be busy. Now Matilda and I would have plenty of time to explore the base of the large hill that sat close to the farmhouse. I was convinced the entrance to Makokoshla mine lay hidden in that hill.

The evening finally came to an end.

I said goodnight to Matilda with an admonition to be up bright and early the next day. We had a mystery to solve.

TREASURE REVEALED.

After a hurried breakfast, we left the house, armed with compass, map and, of course, Matilda's carpetbag. I now had a huge respect for that bag.

Jacob and the inspector had already left for their respective day's work, whilst Robert had gone to oversee some farm business near the dam.

So, the coast was clear as they say.

We walked for a quarter of a mile to get to the base of the hills. The farmhouse was still visible in the distance.

I took out the skin map and a compass that aunt had purloined from Jacob's desk and laid them on the ground.

The thick, black line on the map pointing towards the square with the T in the middle was facing NW. When I lined it up with the farmhouse, left was the direction we had to go.

However, the undergrowth was very thick with thorn bushes.

'These thorns are a blasted nuisance, Ella. Is it my imagination or are there really more bushes than usual? They're growing so thickly together, it's almost impossible to get through. Oh blast it! I'm well and truly stuck.'

And so she was, trapped by thorns as long as three inches entangled in her clothes.

'Hold still. It's going to take a while to free you without ripping your clothes to shreds. I think you're right about there being an exceptional number of thorn bushes in this area. I can only presume they were deliberately planted to stop anyone from randomly exploring this part of the farm, which means we could well be on the right track. But we need a couple of machetes to hack our way through.'

'That will please Jacob.'

'He doesn't have to know about it,' and I freed Matilda from the last thorn that was holding her captive.

'Let's go back to the farmhouse and have a look in the workshop to see if we can find a couple.'

It didn't take us long to retrace our steps.

We found several machetes, of which we took two of the sharpest looking ones as well as a wide beam torch, which would be more effective than the small one we had if we did find the mine entrance.

Before long we were hacking our way through the undergrowth, checking our direction frequently with the compass.

'My arms feel as though they are about to drop off,' panted Matilda. 'This is really hard work.'

'Not for much longer I hope.'

I had glimpsed some promising boulders ahead.

There was one huge boulder flanked by two smaller ones. They looked embedded into the hill, but after creeping around the smaller ones, I could see a gap leading into pitch-blackness.

'It looks like we've found the entrance, aunt. I can just about squeeze myself between these boulders. I'm going to have a look with the torch. I won't be long,' and I disappeared.

Shining the torch around, I could see the boulders had been deliberately placed to conceal the entrance.

I was in a large tunnel with coco pan tracks running away into the darkness. A cold sweat broke out over my body as I couldn't help but remember the previous circumstances of being in a mine.

'Ella! Can you hear me?'

'Yes, aunt. Do you want to take a look?'

'Absolutely,' and there she was, pushing her bag ahead of her as she squeezed herself through the opening.

'Well, well, well. Here we are, back in the mine once again.'

Matilda shivered.

'What do we do now that we've found it?'

'Follow the main line marked on the map to where X marks the spot. We've got the compass points to go by. We've both got torches. Let's go on a treasure hunt.'

With the map and compass leading the way, we followed the coco pan tracks.

Into the hill we went, twisting and turning, following the main tunnel etched on the hide. There were an amazing number of tunnels leading off the one we were in; some, no doubt, dead ends, confusing anyone who might stumble into the mine. Numerous bats flew around our heads as we disturbed their roosting places; their high-pitched squeaking quite deafening.

There was the usual paraphernalia of mining, old lamps hanging on rusty nails, broken shovels and pick axes, over turned coco pans. In fact, it all looked too familiar.

I couldn't help feeling more nervous the deeper we went.

Matilda was unusually quiet. It was obvious she was reliving the horrible experience we had just a few days ago.

The only noise heard was the scuffle of our shoes on the dirt floor and the squeaking of bats.

After walking for an hour, I estimated we were getting close to the other mine entrance. If my calculations were correct, we should be parallel to it within another ten minutes.

'Let's check the map again. The passage we're following stops close to the mineshaft. In fact, it looks as though it comes to an end right under the fig tree. Just a little bit further and we should be there.'

'Thank goodness for that,' exclaimed Matilda. 'After this, I never ever want to go into another mine again. Let's hurry, get to the end of this passage, see if there's anything to find and then get out again quickly,' and Matilda set off, almost at a trot, so eager was she to see the back of this place.

And then we arrived; only to come to an abrupt halt as all that was in front of us was a solid wall of rock.

I shone the torch around, looking for anything out of the ordinary. Nothing! Just solid rock.

I leant against the wall and tried to think if I wanted to hide something in this area of the mine, where would be the best place? X marked the spot on the map, and this was the spot! So, where to look?

'Can you see anything strange or different aunt?'

Matilda was scouring the dirt surface near where we were standing.

'Nothing, nothing at all.'

She sat back on her haunches.

'I was just wondering if, whatever it is we're looking for could be buried. I mean, there's nowhere else to hide anything, is there?'

I joined Matilda and crouched down on hands and knees, carefully making my way around the perimeter, looking and feeling for anything that just didn't seem right.

'Hang on, wait a minute! What's this?'

She was brushing dust and dirt away from an area that astonishingly revealed a wooden box embedded in the floor. It was about eighteen inches square, with a metal groove at one end, and two small rusty hinges at the other.

'We need a hook to catch under the groove to lift it up. It's obviously been here a very long time, and it's stuck.'

'Use my scissors,' and Matilda burrowed into her bag.

I used the blades to scratch around the edges of the wood, creating a small gap.

'Right! That should be enough. Let's see if I can budge it,' and I hooked the blades into the groove and gave a heave. The lid gave way with a jerk revealing a metal container. I was able to open that lid with no problem. Inside, something was wrapped in soft leather.

I carefully lifted the object out of the box. It was very heavy. My heart began beating rapidly. I could hear Matilda catch her breath as she leant closer to see what I was holding. I unwrapped the leather to reveal the most beautiful thing I had ever seen in my life.

It was a peacock, about eight inches in length, made of solid gold, going by the weight of it. Inlaid in the gold, making up the feathers, was a myriad of precious stones; diamonds, emeralds, sapphires, rubies, all cut to give the impression of feathers shimmering with movement as the peacock moved. The eyes were brilliant topaz, the claws, garnet. An elaborate headdress had a black pearl in the centre, with iridescent pearls surrounding it in an ever-widening spiral. The breast was a rainbow of dazzling stones, the diamonds reflecting the colours of the other stones so brilliantly, it literally took our breath away. But the most awesome part of this peacock was hanging from its beak; a carved piece of jade, shaped in the form of a crown, with a flawless diamond cut in a star.

'I can't believe this Ella. That's the Star of David! Turn it over. I must see if anything is carved into the jade.'

Matilda's eyes were glittering, her breath coming in short gasps.

'Yes! There is writing and it's Hebrew. Shine the torch closer. I might be able to decipher it.'

And Matilda began mumbling to herself.

Her voice faded into silence as she concentrated recalling the parts of this ancient language she knew; a language dating back in time thousands of years; a language that had survived pogroms and persecutions; a language that was as resilient as the people who spoke it.

Matilda's lips moved as she silently read the inscription engraved in the jade.

She raised her head and looked at me, eyes sparkling and not just from the reflection of the jewelled peacock.

'Yes! It is as I thought. The Queen of Sheba, who was from Ethiopia, was given this peacock by King Solomon as one of the many personal gifts he gave her when she visited him in Jerusalem, originally known as Salem, when his fame as a wise and great king had spread to other countries, including Ethiopia. There's a record of her visit in the Old Testament of the Bible. Down the ages, there've been rumours of a fabulous, priceless peacock stolen by a courtier, after the Queen of Sheba returned to Ethiopia. People were put to death because of its disappearance, but the peacock was never recovered. It was believed the gold had been melted down, and the precious stones sold.'

Matilda's voice trembled with excitement.

'To think after all these thousands of years, I am holding one of the most prized possessions of the ancient world. It is unbelievable!'

Frankly, I wasn't quite as enamoured as aunt because it was becoming apparent that this could be the object that had been the catalyst of several deaths, and very nearly our own.

No, I was not quite as smitten over the peacock as Matilda. It was very beautiful, though.

The question on my mind was the obvious one.

What do we do next?

'Well,' said aunt, after I voiced my concern, 'the peacock should really be handed over to the Ethiopian Government. After all, it is a national treasure, and belongs to that country.'

'Who do you suggest does the handing over?'

There was a moment's silence.

'Us.'

'Us? You and me? Why?'

'You said yourself, Ella, who can we trust? If this peacock is not delivered into the right hands, the murders will continue. As soon as it's publicly known it's safely housed in the Ethiopian National Museum, the murders will stop.'

'Do you really think so? I suppose you have a point, aunt. But is it worth risking our lives to hand this peacock over ourselves?'

As I said these words, I realised that for Matilda, it was. This was the culmination of years of travel, hoping one day she would make a great find that would leave an imprint on the specialized world of archaeology.

'You don't have to answer, aunt. I can see by your face you'd be willing to risk anything to see this peacock restored to its rightful owners.'

'Yes Ella, I would. But I have absolutely no right in expecting you to get yourself involved to that extent.'

'Are you kidding? I've never been to Ethiopia. My feet are getting itchy, and that feeling of excitement in the pit of my stomach is making itself felt. Ethiopia here we come!'

A huge bear hug was my reward.

I gave the soft leather covering to her, and she gently wrapped the peacock and placed it almost reverently in the depths of her carpetbag.

I lowered the lid of the box and tried to conceal it as best I could. Our footprints in the dust were another matter, but we scuffed them randomly, hoping if they were noticed by anybody, the conclusion would be drawn that nothing had been found, as it was a dead end.

I have to admit all the time we were in the mine; I was listening for sounds telling us we weren't alone. It was nerve wracking. Now the 'treasure' had been found, I wanted out of the place as quickly as possible.

'Let me carry the bag, aunt. That peacock is heavy,' and I hoisted it over my left shoulder, took the map out of my jeans pocket, and began retracing our steps.

The journey back was uneventful.

We arrived at the opening of the mine unhindered, and after squeezing ourselves between the boulders, moved away from the entrance as quickly as possible, and then found a place to sit and savour the fresh air and the sun on our faces.

We couldn't relax for long.

It was already past four o'clock. We had to get to the farmhouse before Jacob arrived back from Gweru.

We quickly walked along the path to the house, replaced the torch and machetes in the workshop, put the compass back on Jacob's desk and hurried to our bedrooms.

After a shower and change of clothes, I was sitting on Matilda's bed, scrutinizing the peacock. It was breathtakingly beautiful.

'So Ella. What's our next step?'

I sat thinking for a moment.

'I'm still puzzling over the connection with Swingen Linen. The scarf they inadvertently gave you seems to be the link but in what way? Also, did Frederick Short and his nephew die because of the peacock, or because they wanted to lay claim to Tevrede?'

I thought for a moment.

'Is Jacob aware of the peacock's existence? No, that doesn't make sense. Surely he would have found it himself if he did. On the other hand, is he aware he could lose the farm? Now that's something he would get really mad about, and who knows to what lengths he would go to make sure he didn't. And then there's Swingen Linen. Where do they fit in, for goodness sake! Are they a front for treasure seekers that would go to any lengths to get their hands on priceless objects?'

I paused for breath, brain buzzing overtime with all the possibilities.

'You know aunt, finding the peacock has uncovered more questions than answers. But of course, the big question is how on earth the peacock ended up in a mine in the southern end of Africa. Ethiopia is right in the north. It must've been carried down through Africa millennia ago. Somehow, Philip's grandfather got hold of it and hid it before he was murdered. But was he murdered because of the peacock, or because he'd won Tevrede in a poker game?'

Matilda chuckled.

'Each question we answer leads to half a dozen more, unanswered. You have to admit, Ella, this whole business gets more and more intriguing.'

It was obvious aunt was still in the euphoric state she'd been in since we'd found the peacock.

I, on the other hand, was apprehensive of what lay in store for us.

I tried not to show aunt my true feelings.

She was on such a high with the peacock's discovery; I didn't have the heart to dampen her spirits. After all, we only had to deliver the peacock to the Ethiopian authorities, and that was that.

Who was I trying to kid...?

There was the sound of a jeep coming along the driveway.

Jacob was returning home.

EXIT.

'Put the peacock back in your carpetbag, aunt. It should be safe there for now. After dinner we'll think of a way to leave Tevrede without arousing suspicions. Inspector Stuart doesn't need us any longer, and we certainly don't want to out stay our welcome, now do we?'

I would have got more response if I'd been talking to the door.

Prising the peacock out of Matilda's hands, I wrapped it in its covering and placed it in her bag.

And not a moment too soon.

A knock on the door had aunt jumping guiltily.

I opened it to find Jacob standing there, a smile on his face.

'I was wondering if you would both like to join me for sundowners in the garden before dinner. It's a lovely evening.'

'We would be delighted, wouldn't we aunt?' and I bustled her out of the door as Jacob led the way.

Sitting under the jacaranda tree, sipping an ice-cold mixture of mango juice and guava, I sat back in my chair enjoying the sounds of Africa, whilst Matilda chattered inconsequentially to Jacob. She's very good at small talk.

The events of the day passed through my mind.

What a day!

Never in my wildest imaginings did I dream we would stumble on something of such international importance.

Whilst pondering over the peacock and its Hebrew inscription, I began to realise the enormous consequences of the discovery, not least in discovering something that would cause major ripples in intellectual circles. We had found proof of a story in the Bible so many people thought was just that, a story; a make believe event that never took place.

On our way out of the mine, Matilda had elaborated on the 'fable' saying she always believed the visit had really happened.

What would the ramifications of this find mean to the Jewish people?

Vindication of some sort?

Was I imagining more importance in the peacock than there really was?

And what about the Ethiopians?

There is a strong Jewish community in Ethiopia. Did their history stem back to those times? Did the Queen of Sheba bring back the Jewish religion to Ethiopia? Did she herself convert to Judaism?

I felt a gentle tap on my arm.

With a jerk I came out of my reverie. Jacob was looking at me with his penetrating eyes.

'Your aunt was telling me what an interesting day you had exploring the bushveld. I would've enjoyed being with you, but hopefully, tomorrow I'll have the opportunity to show you and Matilda the other part of the farm that is as beautiful as that by the dam, although in a different way.'

I blurted out, 'We have to go home!'

So much for not arousing any suspicions. I could've kicked myself! What was I thinking!

Jacob was taken aback, as well he might.

'Ella!'

That was aunt, sounding scandalized.

'I'm so sorry. That sounded very rude. What I meant was we can't impose on your hospitality any more, Jacob. You've been so kind and generous in letting us stay in your home. I don't know what we would've done without you, but it's time we returned to England. I don't think Inspector Stuart needs us any longer, and we've taken up far too much of your time. Aunt and I must start making arrangements tomorrow. We can leave Tevrede early to drive to Harare, and then make sure of our flight back to London...'

My voice trailed away.

Even in the dusk, I could see the emotions flitting across Jacob's face; hurt, disappointment, anger.

His face then assumed the blank, stony look I remembered from the mining office.

'If that's what you want, Ella. You know you and your aunt are welcome to stay at Tevrede as long as you wish. However, if you want to leave tomorrow, I'll see that your car is ready for the journey,' and abruptly pushed his chair back and strode around the side of the house towards the garages and disappeared.

'Don't say anything, aunt. That was unforgivable of me, I know.'

Matilda just nodded her head.

'I have to get away. You do understand, don't you?'

'I understand.'

The noise of crickets was rising to a crescendo, only to stop abruptly as the sound of the dinner gong reverberated through the garden.

'Come, my dear. Let's put on a cheerful face for dinner,' and Matilda tucked her arm into mine, gave it a squeeze, and marched me across the lawn into the house.

No chance to explain.

Dinner was more pleasant than I expected.

Inspector Stuart agreed there was nothing more he needed us for. Investigations were continuing, and he was sure our assailants would be caught very soon, and he would prefer we were back in England, anyway.

Jacob's brother regaled us with an amusing story of a baby warthog that had run amok in the kitchen of one of the neighbouring farms.

Jacob told us about the new mining commissioner who would be starting next month, and how much he was looking forward to being a full time farmer on Tevrede.

But all the while I felt the questioning look in his eyes when they rested on my face.

What could I say? Nothing.

Finally, dinner was finished.

Matilda and I said our goodnights, and made our way to the stairs.

'Ella! Wait one moment please.'

I turned to see Jacob standing at the bottom of the stairs.

'I'll be with you just now, aunt,' and I retraced my steps.

I stopped a couple of stairs up so I could be on the same level as Jacob. One feels at a disadvantage at having to look up at a person all the time.

He put his hands on my shoulders and said,' I want you to know that if you ever need my help with anything, just ask.'

I opened my mouth to speak. He placed a finger against my lips.

'No. Don't say anything. Something has happened that has caused you to put up a barrier between us.'

Jacob stopped talking, obviously trying to find the right words.

'I find it difficult to get close to people, but I felt an immediate affinity with you, even when you and your aunt were invading my space at the mining office. You fascinated me then, and you continue to fascinate me now. I have no idea what has happened to make you feel you can't trust me, but somehow I will prove to you that you can.'

His grip on my shoulders tightened.

I stared into those black eyes that seemed to be searching my very soul. He then planted a fleeting kiss on my lips and without a backward glance, strode towards the front door, opened it, and disappeared into the darkness.

I stood for a few moments, staring at the door, a gamut of emotions running through me.

I turned and ran up the stairs to Matilda's room.

She was in bed, lovingly caressing the peacock.

'You know, Ella. I can understand people who acquire priceless works of art, sitting and gloating in a solitary state, feasting their eyes on their acquisitions.'

She paused long enough to ask me what Jacob wanted.

'Nothing much. Just that we must let him know if we need him for anything.'

I changed the subject.

'Have you any idea how we're going to get that peacock to its rightful destination? I'm thinking of passport controls, luggage going through x-ray units, anything to declare, nothing to declare, you know the sort of thing.'

'Well,' said aunt, carefully folding the peacock in its cloth. 'Just put it in my bag will you,' handing it to me. 'I've been thinking about that very problem, and I do believe I have the answer. Over the years, I've made many friends in the archaeological field, and Professor Henry Mableton is the most prominent. He has worldwide influence. All I need do is ask him to fax me the documents giving permission to carry the relic from one country to another.'

I looked at her doubtfully.

'That seems too easy. Do you think it would work?'

'Why not! Often the simple plan is far more effective than the elaborate one. There's much less that can go wrong.'

She had a point.

'We don't have to elaborate on the find; just some bare details. Henry knows me well. I actually helped him out on a rather delicate situation not so long ago, so, in one way he owes me a favour. I'll carry the peacock in my bag, in a suitable container, all wrapped and sealed; show it to customs with the documents and there we are. Next stop, the Ethiopian Embassy in London, safely delivered.'

'London! I thought we were going to Ethiopia?'

'I've been thinking about that, and really, it's too risky to take that journey, especially as our two friends haven't been caught yet. The sooner it's off our hands the better, although it's going to be such a wrench to hand it over.'

I was disappointed. No! I was very disappointed.

But aunt did have a point.

I gave her a hug, said goodnight and went to my room.

I lay in bed, staring into space, pondering over the words Jacob had spoken.

It was true.

I'd also felt that bond between us, but tried to discount it having had a disastrous relationship in the past, showing my judgment of character was sadly amiss.

But this time was different.

This time I really cared.

To deliver the package.

Tazwhila had kindly topped up the oil in the car, and water in the radiator. The petrol gauge showed full, and our suitcases were stowed in the boot.

Jacob was nowhere to be seen.

We showed our appreciation to the couple in monetary terms and then drove along the drive and out onto the main road leading to Harare.

'I've a feeling this won't be the last we see of Tevrede,' remarked Matilda.

I shook my head, despondency welling up inside, but determined to be upbeat in front of Matilda.

'No aunt. Best to forget this place. Let's concentrate on delivering the peacock to its rightful owners, and get our lives back to normal. I'll definitely write a series of articles for the uni travel mag on the pleasant aspects of our visit, especially Gloria's cooking. Wasn't it mouth-watering?'

And that topic kept the conversation going until we reached the Oasis Motel, stopping for refreshments before driving the rest of the way to the capital.

Pulling up outside the Flamboyant Hotel, the same one we'd stayed in when we arrived in Zimbabwe, Matilda quickly went to reception.

'Do you have a fax machine I can use,' she asked, whilst I signed us in.

'We have one in the office,' and the receptionist pointed towards a door on her right.

'Thank you very much. May I have your fax number please?' and Matilda wrote it down in her diary.

Our luggage was taken to our rooms. After unpacking a few necessities, I went next door, and found aunt talking animatedly on the telephone.

'Yes, Henry. That's exactly what we want. No, I promise you, you'll be the first to see this piece when we get to England...Yes, I realise this is unorthodox, but I'll explain everything when I see you. Then you'll understand why it's so vital we arrange for it to get to England with as little fuss as possible. Oh, many thanks Henry. You really are a dear. Here's the fax number to send copies of the documents I need,' and Matilda rattled off the number. A few more pleasantries were spoken and then aunt replaced the receiver.

She looked at me, a satisfied grin on her face.

'I gave Henry just a tiny inkling of what we'd found. He's always been supportive of my idea that the Queen of Sheba had actually visited King Solomon in Jerusalem. That was enough for him to want to help with no more questions asked. We must show him the peacock before we hand it over. He's in London at the moment, having just returned from a dig in the Holy Land. It was pure providence I was able to reach him. Now, what do we do next?'

'Find a suitable container for the peacock; phone the airport to find out departure times and enjoy what little time we have left in Harare. Have you unpacked anything yet?'

'No. I wanted to get hold of Henry as quickly as possible.'

'Why don't you unpack whilst I phone departures?'

There was a flight leaving for London the following evening. I made reservations for us.

'We should be organised by then. If you've finished unpacking, we'll see if the fax has arrived and get that container. Maybe we should leave the peacock in the hotel's safe for now. I don't think you should carry it around with you. Let's see if reception has a large envelope we could buy. We could put it inside and sellotape it securely.

That done, we entered the office just as Matilda's fax appeared. She read it eagerly.

'This is perfect. We shouldn't have any problems in getting the peacock through with this high level of authorization.'

She tucked the fax into one of the many pockets of her carpetbag.

'Right. Now for the container and then some belated lunch.'

We left the hotel and decided to walk, rather than drive. The sun beating down caused the road to ripple as heat waves did a complicated dance on the tarmac.

I'm going to miss all of this,' I thought, as we crossed the street to eat at a restaurant we'd visited on our first trip to the capital.

There's something very special about Africa. Somehow, the soul of it gets into your blood. I can almost hear the rhythmic drums beating in the distance to some mystical and ancient ceremony starting way back in time. I can see the leopard and lion skins adorning tribal chiefs as they survey their subjects bowing before them. I can smell the sorghum beer bubbling away in large iron pots suspended over wooden fires. I can hear the women singing melodious songs in harmony whilst beating their washing in rhythm on the rocks of the river bank...'

'Ella, Ella' hissed Matilda, shaking my arm. 'Look over there! It's Ken!'

Did I come back to earth with an almighty thump.

We ducked into the doorway of a shop and hid ourselves as best we could.

Ken sauntered along the opposite side of the road, peering into shop windows as though he hadn't a care in the world. Attempting to murder two women obviously didn't give him any sleepless nights. Never did I think our attackers would still be in Africa, let alone jaunting around the streets of Harare. But where was the other one?

'I can't see his accomplice,' said aunt. 'I wonder what's happened to him. We must get to a telephone and speak to Inspector Stuart. I'm sure he said he was staying one more night with Jacob to finish off some business, and then go back to England. The problem is we might lose sight of this thug in the process. Maybe we should follow him and hopefully he'll lead us to his crony. I can't imagine how they've escaped detection from the police. It doesn't make any sense.'

Ken glanced at his watch outside a pavement café, then settled himself in a chair and gave an order to a hovering waiter.

'I wonder if he's waiting for his friend?'

'Most likely,' I replied.

True enough, within five minutes, the other thug arrived.

After sitting down, he proceeded to hog the conversation. Ken sat impassively, listening to every word.

The waiter arrived with two cups of coffee. Ken's accomplice didn't miss a beat in his one sided conversation.

'Whatever he's saying to Ken must be important. They haven't touched their drinks,' observed Matilda.

'I wonder if they know we never died in the mine. All the activity surrounding the place once Inspector Stuart arrived must have set tongues wagging. This could get awkward for us if they've found out we were staying on Tevrede and have left the farm. The obvious thing would be for us to travel to Harare and catch a flight back to England. Do you think they'll have someone watching the airport? They could have checked up on passengers flying to the U.K. and know we'll be on the flight tomorrow evening.'

'And he's probably telling Ken the plan for our demise right now,' said Matilda, matter of factly.

'Then we must give them the slip.'

'How?'

'By not returning to England by plane.'

'How else do you suggest we get home?'

'By travelling overland, up the continent of Africa by land rover.'

Matilda stared at me as though I'd taken leave of my senses.

'Step back more in the doorway, aunt. They've paid the waiter and are leaving.'

Ken went one-way, his friend, the other.

We didn't attempt to follow either of them.

I was convinced the news of our escape from the mine had reached them. The sooner we shook Harare dust off our heels, the better.

'Let's get back to our hotel. We'll phone Inspector Stuart from there, but, we won't tell him our change of plan.'

Matilda was quiet.

She was obviously still digesting the morsel I'd given her about the overland trip.

'Whatever gave you that idea?' she demanded, once I finished talking on the phone.

I replaced the receiver. Inspector Stuart had already left Tevrede.

'I read a post card stuck on the notice board in the foyer, asking if there were two people interested in sharing the expenses of a trip through to the north of Africa in a land rover. Let me pop down and get it.'

Once back in aunt's room, I read the card more thoroughly.

'Are you looking for adventure?

Then this is a must do for you.

Two seats available in a well sprung land rover.

All mod cons needed to give you an exciting trip to the north of Africa without having to rough it too much!'

'Aunt, nobody would expect us to do anything like this. Let's phone this guy and see what he has to offer.'

Matilda agreed.

So, I phoned David Blade on 275-321 and found out he'd put the post card in the foyer only thirty minutes before we checked into the hotel. This must be a good omen.

'We're on our way to meet you,' his booming voice announced, and then the line went dead.

I replaced the receiver and grinned at Matilda.

'David Blade is on his way.'

'Humph!' was Matilda's reply.

THE QUEST CONTINUES.

We ordered room service for coffee and had just poured our second cup when there was a knock on the door.

I peered through the peephole, obviously wary of who was on the other side and then opened it revealing a man of gigantic proportions. He thrust out a hand in greeting.

'I'm David Blade,' and engulfed my hand in his as he energetically pumped it up and down, 'and this is my wife Cynthia.'

Behind this human mountain stepped out an animated doll. She was exquisite, with long black hair and huge blue eyes fringed with the longest lashes I've ever seen.

'Hullo,' she said, in a perfectly modulated voice.

'Hi, I'm Ella. Please come in. This is my aunt Matilda'

David Blade filled the room. Don't get me wrong. He wasn't fat or anything like it. He was just huge, well over six feet tall and a body built to match his height.

He sat on the sturdiest chair in the room whilst his wife perched daintily on the edge of the sofa.

I ordered more coffee from room service, and then listened whilst David Blade expounded on the features of this deluxe land rover, the planned route through Africa to the Mediterranean and the approximate cost of the whole trip.

He'd thought of everything.

I was surprised such a delicate looking creature like Cynthia would've wanted to be part of such a journey, but she obviously adored her giant, and I suppose, that was reason enough.

However, appearances can be very deceptive as I found out on the journey.

Cynthia was made of tensile steel, both mentally and physically, with a huge capacity to remain calm and collected whilst the rest of us, including David, ran around like headless chickens. But that's another story.

Aunt Matilda was showing interest.

I could see by the enthralled expression on her face that the thought of such a trip as this in the capable hands of this gentle giant was appealing to her very much.

I expect you've guessed why I was keen to go.

That's right. Not just to give Ken and co the slip, but to go to Ethiopia itself. When Matilda had vetoed the trip on account of its dangers, I was very disappointed. Now, however, things were totally different. To go the sensible route was far more dangerous to us than this proposed journey.

Yes, it sounds like going to the extreme, I know, but I really didn't want to leave Africa yet. What better way of seeing a continent than to drive through it, with the added goal of delivering the peacock to the Ethiopian authorities.

Does the argument sound a bit thin?

Well, at the time it seemed the right way to go.

Matilda was asking David how long he thought it would take us.

'We can do it in eight weeks, maybe less. I know the state of the Great North Road, which is the main road we'll be taking, is excellent in some places but pretty grim in others. Cynthia and I actually have a date to meet some friends in Cairo in ten weeks. I've done this trip several times before, so I'm well acquainted with what's in store such as drunken border guards and all that sort of thing.'

He looked fondly at his wife.

'Cynthia is determined to go on this trip. That's one of the reasons I was keen to meet you after you'd phoned. It will be nice for my wife to have some female company.'

'Well aunt? What do you think?'

Matilda looked at me and grinned.

'Yes, Ella. This sounds just the way to go.'

I was delighted!

Handshakes were exchanged, the trip toasted with coffee, and David and Cynthia left, leaving us with a list of instructions on what extra things to get, such as sleeping bags and plenty of mosquito repellent.

We arranged to meet outside the hotel at seven am Friday morning.

Today was Wednesday.

A lot of things to do before pick up time, as well as making sure we didn't bump into our 'friends.'

I rang Avis and arranged for the car to be collected. We found a perfect container for the peacock which Matilda lovingly prepared and then settled her prize in the deepest recesses of her carpetbag. Our vaccination certificates were up to date, anti-malarial tablets taken, no problem with passports, bush whacking clothes packed and sleeping bags organised.

We were ready for the great trek!

ANTICIPATION.

Friday dawned bright and clear.

Not a cloud appeared in the sky to dampen our enthusiasm. Ken and co hadn't resurfaced so we optimistically assumed they'd high tailed it out of Africa.

Our remaining belongings were packed, breakfast had been eaten, and we were ready for departure outside the hotel entrance at exactly seven a.m.

David Blade pulled up in the land rover just as we settled our luggage around us.

'A man who is punctual. What a pleasure,' exclaimed Matilda, and she waved to Cynthia, who was leaning out of the front passenger window.

The land rover was all David had said it would be.

This was luxury indeed.

Even with all our paraphernalia packed in, there was plenty of legroom. Two spare tyres were securely fastened on top of the land rover and another at the back. There were four large water containers, six petrol cans, a winch, jack, large toolbox and anything else you could think of to make our journey plain sailing. Food supplies such as tin goods were stowed in containers under our seats. Cooking utensils were packed away in special compartments built into the side of the land rover, which, when opened, folded down into a table with adjustable legs, and plenty of space for the cook. (We were to take turns with that chore.)

After double-checking everything, we were ready to hit the road. The engine raced to life with enough horsepower to take us up Mt. Kilimanjaro.

The mood was buoyant.

Matilda was chatting away to Cynthia about anything and everything whilst David added his bit to the conversation in- between manoeuvring the land rover through the busy streets of Harare.

I sat back in my comfortable seat, and for the first time in ages, really relaxed.

I turned my thoughts to the journey ahead.

Was it going to be too strenuous for Matilda? Somehow, I didn't think so. After what she'd been through lately, a jaunt through Africa would be a piece of cake. Finding the peacock had given her such a huge impetus; she was ready to tackle anything.

As for me?

Well, I was content to go along just for the ride. I would face reality again when it thrust itself in my face. Meanwhile, I was going to enjoy the experience of a lifetime.

I stopped daydreaming.

David was telling us about our first border stop.

'We'll stop at Chirunda, which borders on Zambia and Zimbabwe, and then push on to Lusaka. After that, we head east to Lilongwe in Malawi and make our way up Lake Malawi until we cross into Tanzania. We'll then head for Dar Es Salaam and drive up the coast to Mombasa in Kenya, shoot across to Nairobi and then head north to Ethiopia and Addis Ababa.'

He paused, and turned his head to look at me.

'That's where you and Matilda want to get off, eh Ella?'

I'd told David we had some business to do in Addis Ababa, but hadn't elaborated on what it was.

I nodded.

'If we can sort things out quickly, I hope Matilda and myself will be able to carry on travelling with you as far as Cairo. It would be amazing to travel the length of the Red Sea. In fact, this whole trip will be amazing,' and I smiled.

THE CALM BEFORE THE STORM.

And it was; absolutely amazing.

Not without its mishaps of course. No one can hope to drive a vehicle through Africa without punctures happening along the way, getting stuck whilst crossing muddy river beds, having monkeys and baboons raiding the larder or finding snakes curled up snugly in the bottom of sleeping bags.

We organised a routine.

David and I shared the driving, David dealing with border guards as need be. I did see a fair bit of money changing hands, but as bribery is considered a normal part of life in Africa, it soon became a matter of course. Matilda kept her eye on the map, and Cynthia, apart from always looking as though she'd stepped out of the fashion pages of Vogue, had a terrific knack of remaining incredibly cheerful at all times, regardless of how hot and sticky it was, or how many millions of mosquitoes were on the attack, or how drenched and filthy we were, whilst persuading the land rover to get out of a bed of mud during a tropical down pour. We all had our part to play, and in a strange way, complimented each other.

It was an idyllic time.

The scenery was magnificent, ever changing, large areas of grassland merging with dense tropical vegetation as we moved closer to the equator. We drove over mountain ranges, with waterfalls rivalling the beauty of Victoria Falls in Zimbabwe, and then were plunged into tropical forests with birds and insects of such iridescent colour; it was like seeing jewels darting in and out of the foliage.

We came to a grinding halt in Tanzania as hundreds of migrating animals crossed the dirt road ahead of us. What a spectacle; zebra, antelope, elephant, all slowly making their way along a centuries old trail only they knew about.

We ate local produce along the way, as long as it could be peeled. A type of banana called Matoki came in handy as a substitute for potatoes. This banana is small and hard, so it can be fried, boiled and even roasted. Eggs and peanuts were also part of our staple diet. All water, of course, had to be purified, so tablets were used for that purpose. By listening to David, we avoided a lot of pitfalls other travellers' fall into, including 'gippo guts.'

There were some officious border guards who insisted on their hands being liberally greased, but once into the interior, the local population were very hospitable. We even had a show of musical talent put on by school children as a thank you after David helped fix the generator of a rural high school in Tanzania. These young people have such a sense of rhythm with their drum beating and dancing, I felt myself caught up in the mood, and before long, I was moving with the best of them.

The days merged into weeks.

Matilda and I were tanned and fit. The spartan diet suited us, although I would be lying if I didn't say I missed Gloria's cooking now and again.

We met an amazing variety of people on the way; Irish Catholic nuns dedicating their lives to helping Africans suffering from leprosy; Japanese electronic experts helping to bring Tanzania into the space age; a grizzled Yorkshire man captaining the ferry on Lake Malawi.

What a magical trip that was, drinking sundowners in the middle of the lake, watching a fiery sunset whilst being serenaded by roaring lions.

We met game rangers dedicated to the conservation of endangered species, and witch doctors or sangomas, who threw the bones to tell us our future. Mine was murky.

At the end of five weeks we passed through a small town called Shimani on the Tanzanian, Kenyan border, and made our way along the coast to Mombasa.

Sparkling blue sea, white as snow sand and swaying palm trees greeted us as we drove towards the town. There was a strong Indian feel to the place, permeated with Moslem overtones. Men wearing fezzes and women in saris were the norm. It was very cosmopolitan with a cacophony of languages being spoken.

I was fascinated, and would love to have stayed longer. However, David was keen to get to Nairobi to spend a few days overhauling the land rover and replenishing supplies for the journey into Ethiopia.

From Mombasa we drove northwest to Nairobi, the Kenyan capital. What a beautiful city, with many reminders of colonial times visible in the buildings that had an old world aura about them. These were tucked in-between modern skyscrapers denoting a city as modern as any in the world. Easy to forget one was in Africa until a very tall Masai warrior with ochre reddened face walked stately by, followed by his retinue of wives and children.

'Here we are, ladies,' said David, pulling up outside the majestic Kenyatta hotel.

'I think showers, a huge carvery with trimmings, and then soft beds are on the menu eh?'

He cupped Cynthia's exquisite face in his huge hands.

'You really are a glorious travelling companion, my love,' and kissed her gently as if she were made of rare porcelain china.

David turned in his seat.

'And you ladies. Cynthia and I couldn't have had better companions. We've done really well to reach Nairobi in the time we have. Getting to Addis Ababa will seem like a Sunday jaunt.'

Everything had gone incredibly well.

The valet showed David where to park the land rover, whilst the rest of us trooped into the hotel, looking, and probably smelling, of well-seasoned travellers.

The receptionist took our particulars, gave us room keys and we followed the porter and our luggage to our respective rooms.

The time was five-thirty pm.

'David and I will see you in the dining room, say, at seven. Will that give you enough time?'

'Plenty, and David was right; you are a glorious travelling companion,' and Matilda gave Cynthia a big hug before following the porter to her room.

'I'll pop in after my shower, aunt'.

The bed looked incredibly inviting.

It was all I could do to stop myself flopping on it and sinking into oblivion.

However, a long, hot shower revived me. I put on one of my prettiest dresses, which seemed strange after wearing shorts and T-shirts for weeks. A dab of make-up, a spray of favourite perfume, and I was knocking on Matilda's door.

'Come in,' she called cheerfully, and I walked in to find her putting the finishing touches to her hair.

'My, Ella. How pretty you look. It's nice to be back in civilization. I'll never take my creature comforts for granted again,' and Matilda gave one last pat to her hair, hooked her arm into mine, and we sallied forth to look for the dining room.

Cynthia and David were waiting for us at the bar, and after ordering large refreshing fruit juices, carried our drinks to the table, prepared to do full justice to the delicious meal that lay ahead.

It was hard to choose from the huge variety on the menu.

Eventually Matilda settled on Chicken Doo Piyaza, whilst David went for a curried fish dish called Mtuza Was Samaki. Cynthia fancied Maharagwe, which consisted of spiced red beans in coconut milk, and I chose Kuku na Nazi which is chicken also cooked in coconut milk.

A variety of exotic fruits of the area, mfenesi, nanasi and mabahora were a delicious dessert to complete a gorgeous meal.

We sat chatting for a while over coffee and then the lure of those soft beds waiting for us proved too strong to resist.

BACK TO REALITY.

Aunt and I discussed our itinerary at breakfast.

David was keen on showing Cynthia his favourite haunts, so they'd already left by the time we reached the dining room.

Matilda also wanted to explore, but I was reluctant.

'I don't know why but I feel we need to stay in the hotel for the next few days,' I said to aunt, but she was devouring a tourist guide of the city the receptionist had given her.

'Really, Ella! You don't think those two could have tracked us here do you?'

The excitement of the journey along with the hard slog of travelling seemed to have pushed Ken and co right out of her mind.

'No, I'm sure they haven't, but I'll feel a lot easier once we're back on the road. Maybe I'm becoming paranoid, but that peacock is worth taking risks. How do we know they are the only ones hunting it down? Remember how shocked we were to find them still in Harare when we thought they would've been miles away? No, I'm not underestimating them at all. Also, there's another thing that's worrying me.'

I paused, not too sure how to say what I wanted to say, and then took the plunge.

'Cynthia and David know nothing about the peacock or our being attacked. I've been feeling guilty at the fact we could be involving them in danger, and they're totally unaware of it. That's not right aunt, and you know it.'

'Yes, I have to agree.'

We sat in silence for a while.

'We have another choice you know,' said aunt.

'I think I know what you're going to say. Get a plane from Nairobi to Addis Ababa.'

'Yes. If we do that, Cynthia and David are no longer involved, and I've still got those authorization documents, so getting the peacock through customs shouldn't be a problem.'

'It doesn't seem fair though, to leave them in the lurch. Goodness, what to do! I don't think David will manage all the driving on his own and we did come in handy when the land rover got stuck.'

I thought for a moment.

'No aunt, I'm just getting paranoid. We'll spend a couple of days sight-seeing in Nairobi, and then continue the journey to Ethiopia. Yes, we'll keep to the arrangements. By the way, did you put the peacock in the hotel safe?'

'All safe and snug,' Matilda replied.

'One more cup of coffee then. Where should we go first in exploring Nairobi?'

'Oh, I believe there is an excellent museum I would love to visit,' and I let Matilda rattle off a list of places she wanted to see before we left the city.

The past catches up.

After visiting the Nairobi National Museum aunt had mentioned, we caught a taxi to the Uhuru Gardens and monument built in remembrance of the struggle for independence, granted in 1963. We then spent a delightful afternoon sampling the different coffees Kenya is famous for.

The next day saw us at the Sheldrick Elephant Orphanage, which is close to the Nairobi National Park. Baby elephant and rhino orphaned by poachers killing off the adults for rhino horn and ivory are taken care of by dedicated staff.

That evening, dressed up to the nines, we ventured forth to the theatre with David and Cynthia and watched a local production of Ipi Tombi, which had our hands clapping and feet stomping. Mama Themba's Wedding song was the hit of the evening.

It was a delightful interlude, and we were chatting away, extolling the virtues of the musical as we walked into the hotel, only for Matilda and I to stop dead in our tracks when we saw the back view of Ken and cohort arguing with the receptionist.

'I'm sorry sir, but it's against hotel policy to give out the names of any guests who are staying here!'

We didn't wait to hear anymore.

I touched David's arm to catch his attention, put my finger to my lips and walked straight out of the hotel.

Once outside, David said, 'Hey Ella! What's going on?'

I pointed to a late night café and charged across the road. We slipped through the door and made our way to the back of the café where there were secluded booths.

'Phew! That was close,' gasped Matilda. 'I don't think they saw us, Ella. What do you think?'

'No, I don't think so,' and I glanced at David and Cynthia, who, obviously, were looking somewhat bewildered.

'Let's get some coffee first,' and gave an order for four strong coffees to a hovering waiter.

I then looked at Matilda.

'They really do have a right to know aunt.'

She nodded in agreement.

'Yes, of course they do.'

'Know what, Ella?' asked David, sounding just a tad impatient.

'Well, we haven't been strictly candid with you.'

And I plunged into the story of the first body found in Matilda's cottage, up to nearly walking into Ken at the hotel. There were a number of interruptions by my attentive audience, but three coffee cups later I stopped talking.

'Well I never! This is amazing,' exclaimed David. 'And the peacock? Where is it now?'

'Sealed tightly in a box in the hotel safe.'

David slowly shook his head.

'So that's why you want to get to Addis Ababa; to give the peacock to the Ethiopian authorities.'

'Yes. We didn't know whom we could trust, you see. Things just didn't add up, starting off with Inspector Stuart knowing Jacob, and then those two walking around Harare as brazen as could be, when a massive police hunt was supposed to be tracking them down. Going to England by plane was definitely out. And then seeing your postcard, well, it seemed too good an opportunity to miss.'

'We would understand if you said no more travelling with us,' added Matilda.

'Ella and I have been concerned we could be endangering you, although we didn't expect to see those horrible men turn up at the hotel. However, they have tracked us down, so I suppose this is where we part ways.'

She paused, obviously feeling quite emotional, and then said, 'David, Cynthia, I speak on behalf of Ella as well, when I say it's been delightful knowing you, and trust you'll continue safely on your journey to Cairo.'

'Are you kidding!' interrupted David, excitement reverberating in his voice.

He turned to his wife.

'What do you say, Cynthia? Shall we help them get the peacock to Addis Ababa?'

'Oh yes,' she said sweetly, 'I wouldn't have it any other way.'

'Good girl,' and after giving her a hug, David turned to us and said, 'Right. It's all settled. Next stop, Ethiopia.'

'But are you sure? Those men will stop at nothing to get their hands on that peacock, or to kill us. I would never forgive myself if anything happened to you.'

'Now Matilda, this is our decision,' said Cynthia gently.

She turned to her husband.

'What we have to find out, David is whether those two men are still at the hotel, and if they are how to get Ella and Matilda in and out again without being seen, as well as getting the peacock from the safe. Hopefully, they've left without finding out anything, so the coast should be clear, as they say in the movies,' and she gave her delightful laugh, tucked her hand into her husband's and said, 'Come David, let's see what we can find out. You two stay here until we get back. We don't want those men catching sight of you. Have some more coffee,' and she and David left the coffee shop.

'Have some more coffee! I've drunk so much I'm high on all the caffeine that's buzzing around my brain. Well, what do you think aunt?'

'I'm not sure. Let's wait and see what happens.'

So, wait we did.

After what seemed like hours, but was in fact only forty-five minutes, David and Cynthia returned.

'Seems as though we're in luck. Your two friends left the hotel in a hurry after the receptionist threatened to call the police and have them up on a harassment charge. At least, that's what she told Cynthia. Anyway, there was no sign of them.

We found the tradesmen's entrance and service lift, so getting you into the hotel shouldn't be a problem. Obviously, the sooner we leave Nairobi the better, so I suggest we go as soon as we're ready. I've settled our accounts at the desk, and the night clerk has the keys to the safe. I've given reception the impression we are leaving early tomorrow morning. Right, let's make sure the coast is clear and duck inside the tradesmen's entrance.'

Once that was safely negotiated, we hurried to our rooms and packed our belongings.

David went to the reception desk with Matilda and she retrieved the peacock. She carefully put the sealed box in the bottom of her carpetbag and said, 'Right. That's everything sorted. Are you ready Ella?'

'All packed and raring to go.'

There was a knock on the door, and Cynthia's face appeared.

'David's gone for the land rover. He said he'd meet us outside the tradesmen's entrance in ten minutes. Are you ready to leave?'

We both said yes in unison.

'That means good luck for us, Ella,' and Matilda picked up her luggage and made for the door. I followed suit, and soon we were walking quickly but quietly through the carpeted corridors towards the tradesmen's entrance, where David was waiting for us. We loaded the luggage and then proceeded to make a quiet and sedate getaway.

'Don't want to attract any undue attention,' he said.'

FLIGHT.

The most direct route to Ethiopia from Nairobi is to travel north to Nyeni and continue to Marsabit in Kenya, and then head slightly west to Moyale, which is on the Kenyan border with Ethiopia. From there, we had to drive to Mega Yabelo and go through the Nechisan National Park before heading to Nazret and finally Addis Ababa.

It sounded easy when we discussed it, but I couldn't help wondering how soon Ken and co would catch up with us. Surely they would have the border posts watched. They could even be following us already. The other members of the party didn't seem particularly concerned, so I kept my fears to myself.

We left the hotel around midnight, so by six in the morning, we'd put a fair bit of distance between Nairobi and ourselves.

The sky lightened, casting long, grey shadows on a landscape of undulating plains that appeared to be swaying until I realised we were driving through the renowned Savannah grasslands, home to the majestic Masai tribe, whose introduction into manhood, is killing a lion with just a spear!

Then the sun appeared, and the grey was replaced by shimmering gold, the sun's rays catching the tips of the long grass swaying in the breeze. One could see for miles, now and again glimpsing mud and thatch homesteads of Masai families.

We continued driving, putting as much distance as we could between Nairobi and ourselves. Every so often, I noticed David having a look in the rear view mirror.

I also kept looking behind me, until Matilda told me in testy voice to stop fidgeting like a flea-ridden cat.

I apologized, and tried to relax.

It wasn't easy.

Knowing the extreme lengths those two would go to get their hands on the peacock, I was sure our flight from Nairobi wouldn't be much of a deterrent.

At midday David pulled the land rover off the side of the road and parked it behind a screen of tall gum trees.

'That should keep us from being seen from the road whilst we brew coffee and have a bite to eat.'

The smell of sizzling bacon soon permeated the air, causing stomachs to rumble and mouths to water.

'I didn't realise how hungry I was,' said Matilda, just before popping a loaded fork into her mouth.

'The excitement of the chase,' remarked Cynthia, delicately slicing a piece of bacon.

Nothing seemed to faze her.

Whilst eating, David and I scanned the map looking for a shorter route to the border.

'I'm a bit wary about going too far off the beaten track. I know we need to keep ahead, but I would hate to drive into some sort of dead end.'

'It's possible they've guessed we would head for the border, so they've probably got that covered. I wish we could sneak into Ethiopia without having to advertise our presence.'

'Maybe you can. There are still camel caravans crossing borders in remote places, including Kenya to Ethiopia. In fact, I've known a camel owner for years who lives in Kalacha, which isn't far from the border. We met when I drove one of his sons to hospital. He's always maintained I saved the boy's life and officially made me a member of the clan. I had to go through a ritual involving the whole family, and very nearly ended up married to one of the cousins! Luckily, I had a friend with me who understood the lingo, and called a halt to the proceedings at the crucial moment. However, Ackbar and I have remained close. When we reach Kalacha, smuggling you and Matilda over the border won't be a problem.

Cynthia and I will continue in the land rover as decoy. If your two assailants stop us, we'll tell them a cock and bull story about dropping you off somewhere, and they'll go haring off in another direction. Meanwhile, we'll meet up with you at a predetermined place and then continue on to Addis Ababa.'

'What a brilliant idea!' exclaimed Matilda. 'Just like Lawrence of Arabia. We can dress up in those long flowing robes, and make our way sedately through the desert, part and parcel of a camel train. That will be a wonderful adventure.'

I had to admit the plan had possibilities.

'Okay, I'm for it. But we must hurry to Kalacha; otherwise none of us will be going anywhere.'

We packed up, and were soon making good time.

Dusk descended rapidly.

We'd passed the town of Nyeri, which was nestled in a mountainous area, and were descending at a steady rate, heading towards a large river, which could be seen snaking through the plain ahead of us.

'If we camp by the river tonight, we should reach Kalacha by tomorrow evening, barring any mishaps,' said David.

'You don't think we should keep going? I'll take over driving so you can get some rest.'

'No Ella. Thanks for the offer, but the going gets very rough the closer we get to the border. There are potholes that could easily swallow the land rover whole if we landed in one. Rather we try and get a good night sleep and start at daybreak.'

'I think we should take turns being on watch though,' said Cynthia. 'It would be very unpleasant to be caught by surprise by those two men.'

'Good idea,' said Matilda. 'I'll do first watch; Ella you do second, Cynthia third, and by the time it's David's turn, it will be time to leave anyway.'

By now, we'd reached the river. It was called Ewaso Ngiro, and looked as though it could be crocodile infested, so nobody ventured too close.

David drove the land rover into a thicket, camouflaging it well. We heated tomato soup on the Primus, rather than light a campfire. We didn't want flames giving our position away.

The soup, which happened to be my favourite, was delicious eaten with crusty bread rolls Matilda had bought on the way.

Then, as we relaxed over a cup of coffee, we heard it; a droning sound in the distance, getting closer and closer.

No mistaking the sound of a helicopter. Was it looking for us? Could be!

Grabbing our folding chairs and anything else we could carry, we dived into the land rover.

As night had settled in, the helicopter's searchlight was glowing as the pilot weaved in and out of the trees that followed the riverbank.

'I bet they are searching for us!' exclaimed Matilda.

'Don't worry. I've hidden the land rover well. They'll never find us,' reassured David.

The helicopter criss crossed the area for about ten minutes, before giving up and moving down river, where it was swallowed up in the darkness, the droning of the rotors receding in the distance.

'Do we stay here David, or should we risk journeying on?' asked Cynthia.

'I think we'll stay here for now. We can't be certain it was them looking for us, although I admit it's highly likely. I can't think where they were able to get hold of a helicopter unless they drove to Nyeni and hired one from there. I know there's a small airport used for domestic flights and game viewing at that town.'

I think we'd better get some sleep,' said Matilda.

'Come David. You get yourself comfortable, while we take turns keeping watch.'

Thankfully, the night passed peacefully.

Narrow escape.

By 5am we were back on the rapidly deteriorating road. The full tarmac had long ago given way to the strip affair, and even that had disappeared, to be replaced with a track hacked out through the bush.

'Reminds me of the roads in Tanzania,' said Matilda, gripping tightly to the window straps to prevent herself being thrown around. I was doing likewise.

We bumped along in this manner for several hours until we saw buildings ahead.

'That's Marsabit. Look out for a signpost to Kalacha Dida, and also a garage. I'd better fill up the tank,' said David.

Marsabit was your average dusty African dorp, set in the middle of nowhere.

There were plenty of shanty shacks made of corrugated iron and any other type of material that could be used for shelter. Small children ran towards the land rover with hands outstretched. Street vendors waved their wares of mangoes, pineapples and prickly pears in the air to attract our attention.

'Ridiculous to think we could enter this town quietly, with all this commotion going on,' complained Matilda. 'If Ken and co are already here, they'll soon be aware of our presence.'

'There's a garage up ahead. We'll fill up and get out of here quickly.'

Within fifteen minutes, we were back on track again, having seen a signpost to Kalacha Dida pointing northwest, just outside of town.

We were only five miles from Kalacha Dida when disaster happened.

The front right tyre exploded with a loud bang, and we lurched towards a ditch that loomed alarmingly close, before David could bring the land rover to a halt.

Muttering some rather choice words, he got out to examine the damage. The rest of us did the same.

'Standing here looking at the puncture is not going to get it fixed,' admonished Matilda. 'We've had enough practice changing wheels. Let's get going.'

Like a well-drilled team, we each of us jumped to our respective jobs, organizing the jack, spare wheel etc., whilst David busied himself loosening bolts where the rubber of the tyre was hanging in shreds.

He was tightening the bolts of the new one when, in the distance; the droning of a helicopter could be heard.

'Oh no!' yelled Matilda. 'They're back again!'

'Quick,' shouted David. 'Everyone back in the land rover.'

We piled in and David pulled off the side of the road and made a beeline for a large overhanging rock that was part of a gorge running parallel to the dirt road, about three hundred yards away.

I was desperately looking to see which direction the helicopter was coming, when I heard a pinging sound, then another.

'Good gracious. They're shooting at us. How dare they!'

This from Matilda.

The sound of breaking glass showed one bullet had found its mark. Luckily, it was only a side mirror, but much too close for comfort.

The helicopter over shot us, which meant David could swing the land rover under the overhang before it turned and started taking pot shots at us again.

'Everyone under the land rover. I'm going to get my rifle!' yelled David, as we screeched to a halt.

We tumbled out and slithered on our bellies under the protection of the vehicle.

David's rifle. I'd forgotten all about it. It was powerful enough to bring down an elephant. Would it be enough to scare away a helicopter?

The time it took for the helicopter to turn and head straight at us again was time enough for David to take the rifle out of its case, cock it, and aim.

I watched as he squinted into the scope, and slowly squeezed the trigger. The bullet smashed into the windscreen on the pilot's side, causing the machine to weave wildly. I could clearly see Ken gesticulating madly at the pilot who was desperately trying to regain control of the chopper as it pitched from side to side.

He managed to pull up sharply and then they disappeared over the overhang.

We waited a few minutes to see if they were coming back, but the pilot had obviously had enough.

'That gave them a fright,' said Matilda, and we scrambled to our feet.

'What wonderful shooting! Well done, David.'

Our hero was grinning from ear to ear.

He enjoyed that, I thought, as Cynthia gave her husband a big hug.

A large wink over Cynthia's shoulder at me showed I was right.

'Let's get going,' said David, and he ushered us into the vehicle, before reversing out of the overhang, and making for the dirt road again.

'The sooner we get to Ackbar the better.'

After such an adrenaline rush, the last few miles to Kalacha seemed very tame by comparison.

Matilda was looking worried.

'Ella,' she whispered, 'I really think we must leave David and Cynthia. This isn't fair on them.'

'I heard that Matilda,' said David. 'You're stuck with us, isn't she Cynthia?'

'But of course.'

I looked at aunt, shrugged my shoulders, and smiled.

David had told us Ackbar lived with his family, which included uncles, aunts, cousins, the whole tout, about two miles east of the town, on a desert plain by an oasis called Betua.

'We'll head there first, explain the situation to Ackbar, and once you and Matilda are organised, Cynthia and I will drive into Kalacha and report being chased and fired on by a helicopter for no apparent reason.'

He turned his head to grin at us.

'If we can get the authorities to start poking their noses into Ken's business, it should prove to have a delaying effect on his activities.'

Buildings of Kalacha loomed ahead.

The terrain had gradually changed from dense vegetation to a dry, cruel landscape of mountainous ranges and gorges, tucked between huge flattish areas of stone, with, now and again, a bit of sand thrown in. This was not your typical sand dune type of desert. It looked very forbidding.

David veered off into the desert before reaching the town, and we bumped along for about half an hour, when over the next rise, nestled in between huge boulders, was the oasis of Betua. Scattered around swaying palm trees and a surprisingly large expanse of water, were the low-lying tents of Ackbar's family. Smoke drifted up in numerous trails from the many campfires burning. Dusk was falling, so I supposed the evening meal was being prepared.

We stopped outside one of the larger tents.

By this time, interested spectators were gathering to see who was arriving.

A huge man, almost rivalling David in height and girth, came out of the entrance of the tent, stopped and looked in amazement, before throwing his arms out wide.

'David!'

David yelled, 'Ackbar!'

Hugs were exchanged, introductions made, and then we were ceremoniously escorted into Ackbar's tent.

I noticed Matilda clutching her carpetbag tightly to her chest.

I heard the sound of the land rover being driven off and looked at David.

'It's being hidden,' he explained.

The interior of the tent was a revelation.

From its grey-brown exterior, one would never have guessed the huge kaleidoscope of colour dazzling the eye upon entering.

The tent appeared larger than it looked from the outside, richly adorned with Persian carpets, not just on the floor, but used as wall hangings as well. Numerous brass and copper oil lamps flickered, their muted light giving everything a surreal feeling about it.

Sitting cross-legged on the carpets, drinking strong coffee in tiny porcelain cups with no handles, the kind of coffee that leaves a thick sludge in the bottom, (just like Turkish coffee according to Matilda), we waited as David explained in Arabic our situation to Ackbar. Finally, an arrangement was made, and Ackbar agreed to us travelling on the next camel train, which, luckily, was leaving in the morning. David and Cynthia would report the helicopter incident, and then make their way across the Ethiopian border. We would meet up with them at a town called Mega. According to Ackbar, it would take the camel train approximately ten to fourteen days to do the journey.

'You didn't tell him too much, did you,' asked Matilda anxiously. 'I wouldn't like the whereabouts of the peacock to become common knowledge.'

'No, I was discretion itself. I told him a couple of men are after you because of a murder in England, and you know they're waiting for you at the border. Don't worry, Matilda. Ackbar and his family will guard you and your possessions with their lives.'

'I hope it doesn't come to that,' she replied, and glanced worriedly at the head of the clan.

After a delicious meal of curried mutton with turmeric rice, we were shown to our tent, which had hanging curtains, making partitions for privacy. Thin mattresses were unrolled for bedding, complete with quilted cylinder shaped pillows, which even had tassels dangling from either end.

Very Ali Baba!

After saying goodnight to the others, I put my head on the pillow and didn't stir until a commotion sounding like a hundred wailing banshees brought me awake with a jolt in the morning.

SHIPS OF THE DESERT.

'What on earth is that noise,' grumbled Matilda from behind her curtain.

'Let's go and have a look,' and I scrambled off the mattress and quickly pulled on jeans and t-shirt.

We peeped out of the tent opening, and beheld a spectacle.

At least a hundred camels that had been tethered behind large rocks near the oasis during the night were now kitted up and bellowing their displeasure at having to carry large wooden crates either side of their saddles. These crates hid a variety of goods to sell in Ethiopia, ranging from carpets, spices, jewellery, exotic material, ornaments, in fact, anything that Ackbar could get his hands on and sell for a profit. Contraband goods were probably part and parcel of the whole scheme of things as well.

Whilst watching the activity, we noticed tents around us being struck and folded, ready for loading.

'Ours will be next,' said Matilda. 'Let's pack our belongings and get out of here before we get folded up with the tent.'

We'd no sooner done that when half a dozen of Ackbar's male relatives came into the tent, and with a maximum amount of noise and arm waving, had the tent and everything else packed up and on a camel in less than five minutes.

Matilda and I were standing by our luggage, feeling slightly foolish, when David and Cynthia appeared.

'Good. I see you're ready to leave,' said David. 'Ackbar has picked two good-tempered camels for you to ride if there is such a thing, which from my personal experience, there isn't. However, come with me and we'll get your luggage tied on. Oh yes, he also asked one of his sisters to give you each a long robe and headdress. He wants you to blend in with everybody else.'

Whilst David was talking, we followed him with our luggage, Matilda again glued to her carpetbag.

Ackbar was standing under a palm tree, holding the reigns of two camels.

'Good morning ladies,' he said, in excellent English. 'I trust you slept well?'

'Perfectly,' answered Matilda. 'Ella and I would again like to thank you so much for all your help. I do hope we are not inconveniencing you too much?'

'There is nothing I wouldn't do for my brother David, and if that means helping you avoid a murderer, then so be it.'

He nodded his head at the camels.

'Here are your rides. This one is Molly,' and he pointed to the larger of the two, who looked at me with a decided malevolent look in her eye, 'and this is Prudence.'

I had to smile at the very prim and proper English names these two ladies of the desert had.

'One of my daughters loves reading your English novels, especially by lady authors. I believe the Bronte sisters are her favourites at the moment.'

He waved a hand at the two camels.

'Hence, their names,' and shook his head sadly.

Matilda attempted to get acquainted with Prudence, who just curled her lip in a disdainful way, and continued nibbling daintily on a palm leaf.

Maybe these names weren't so misplaced after all.

After donning long black robes and headdresses, we said our goodbyes to David and Cynthia, wishing each other good luck and reiterating the time and place of our rendezvous with them in Ethiopia.

Molly and Prudence were persuaded to go down on their knees and we scrambled on to their backs. After a lot of grunting and probably cursing in camel language, they slowly got to their feet and began to sway. I hung on to the toggle with a vice like grip; scared I was literally going to be swayed off. The ground seemed a long way down.

'I can see why these animals are called Ships of the Desert. I'm going to be sea sick,' I gasped to Matilda, who appeared perfectly at ease on Prudence.

'Oh, I'm sure you'll find your sea legs soon,' she shot back instantly.

'That was witty for so early in the morning.'

Nevertheless, I did become proficient at swaying in unison with Molly, and she definitely became better tempered for it, only now and again nipping the rear end of the camel in front of us.

The camel train was a spectacular sight.

Although the vast majority of women wore black, the men and camels themselves were decked out in brightly coloured costumes and camel gear. Tassels in red, gold and orange hung from every conceivable place, so, with the camels swaying, the tassels swaying and passengers swaying, we looked like a very long snake slithering its way through this inhospitable land.

It was hot, very hot, with temperatures soaring to forty degrees plus.

I was extremely grateful for the robe and headdress, because surprisingly, it deflected a lot of heat.

I glanced at Matilda.

She was in her element. No, there wasn't any need to be worried about her for now.

We'd been riding for an hour or so, when a boy of about twelve years old ran up to us.

'You want? You want?' he asked, holding out a small container to each of us.

I reached down and grabbed mine quickly before I slipped out of the saddle.

It was a container full of dried figs, which were delicious, especially when washed down with the sweet water we drank out of the skin water bags.

Fisal was one of Ackbar's many grandsons. He attached himself to us; keeping us supplied with food and water, particularly water, during the long hot journey.

By four in the afternoon, I was feeling stiff from the ride, and breathed a sigh of relief when we stopped at a small oasis named Tribut.

The camels were unloaded and allowed to drink their fill at the watering hole. Meanwhile tents were unpacked and quickly erected. Fisal helped us with our luggage and organised the mattresses, pillows and curtain partitions. Soon, the smell of cooking pervaded the air, and we had the honour of eating with Ackbar and his immediate family.

The men were always served first by their women, who blended in the background. We tried talking to these ladies, but they were very shy, giggling a little behind their veils and then melting away.

However, chatting with Sophie, Ackbar's daughter, who enjoyed reading the Bronte sisters, was a joy. She was so enthusiastic for the classics we had a great discussion on their merits. I had a couple of paperbacks I'd been carrying around with me, so gave them to her. She was delighted, and told me she would treasure them forever.

The days merged into one another.

The routine was to start early, whilst it was still cool, and make as much progress as possible, before the heat of the day caused people and animals alike to slow down and stop.

Soon I was riding Molly like an old hand. She even responded to my commands, so I could save Fisal having to lead her everywhere.

Matilda flourished. She handled the heat well, and the slow rhythmic movement of the caravan suited her admirably.

The arid mountainous land didn't change much.

It was very beautiful in its own unique way, sometimes breathtakingly so, when the early morning rays of the sun brought out the ochre red of the rock intermixed with the fawn yellow of the sandstone. The elements had done a fantastic job carving incredible shapes in the rocks, and my imagination had full reign in the slow pace we were traveling, to see cathedrals, towers and castles carved in them.

The sunsets were just as amazing, the whole spectrum of colours present, ranging from pale pink to vivid gold as the sun set, then revealing a multitude of stars that seemed so close, I could put out a hand and pluck them from the sky.

There were days when it became very windy, but as it wasn't a sandy desert, we didn't really suffer too much discomfort from swirling sand.

Ackbar and his family treated us very well. We always ate with him and the rest of the clan. Fisal was our official minder who smoothed the way for us.

So consequently it was easy to forget the reason for being part of this camel train. The memory of brutality chasing us receded into the distant recesses of our minds, as we gave ourselves up to the timelessness of this type of travel.

Ambush.

Towards the end of the second week, I noticed a certain tension in the air.

We were heading towards a deep gorge, the sides of the sheer cliffs rising up steeply on either side. The trail was extremely narrow, only wide enough for single file.

Rifles appeared as if by magic, and all talking ceased, the only noise being the shuffling and snorting of the camels. Even the children sensed they had to be quiet.

I turned in my saddle to speak quietly to Matilda.

'What's going on, aunt?'

'Bandits.'

'I beg your pardon?'

'Bandits. As you can see, this is an ideal place for an ambush,' and she put her finger to her lips.

I swivelled back in my saddle.

She has to be joking!

If that was the case, why on earth were we riding through the gorge in the first place! Couldn't we ride around it? How ironic to escape from one type of violence, only to be killed by bandits robbing this camel train!

We were towards the end of the caravan, so the front-runners had long disappeared into the gorge by the time we began ambling through.

Then we heard them; gun shots ringing out, echoing loudly in the confines of the gorge, immediately followed by loud shouting from the men, screaming from the women, and crying from the children.

'Oh great!' and I jerked round to yell at Matilda to turn Prudence so we could get out.

Fisal grabbed hold of the reins and yanked hard on Prudence's head, turning her so sharply she didn't have time to protest.

Molly saw what was happening to her sister, and thankfully, followed suit.

The commotion caused Prudence to bolt back out of the gorge with Molly in fast pursuit. Fisal was hanging on to the reins for dear life. Matilda managed to grab him under an arm and drag him on board.

We shot out of that gorge like two corks out of champagne bottles.

My attention was riveted on staying in the saddle. I had no ideal camels could run so fast.

We galloped for ages, the camels totally uncontrollable, until eventually, Prudence began slowing down, helped by Matilda and Fisal frantically pulling on the reins. Molly followed suit, and soon they were trotting, then walking, and finally came to a standstill, trembling with excitement and fatigue.

They nuzzled one another.

'All in one piece, aunt?'

'I think so. Thank goodness our luggage was strapped on tightly. The carpetbag is safe.'

I looked at Fisal.

He was sitting absolutely rigid in front of Matilda. She gave him a big hug and told him not to worry, we would catch up with the rest of the family, and she was sure they were all fine.

Fisal managed a wobbly grin and nodded.

Matilda turned to me.

'You don't think Ken and co had anything to do with the ambush, do you Ella?'

'I'm not sure…No, surely not. Could just be a coincidence. It's obvious something similar has happened before. The clan were obviously prepared for some sort of tussle occurring.'

Molly and Prudence, having finished nuzzling each other, clearly wanted to get moving again.

We looked around.

The landscape appeared the same, and yet different, if that makes any sense. There was no sign of any of the other camels. In fact, we seemed to be the only living things for miles.

'I don't recognize any of this,' sweeping my arm in a wide arc. 'I hope Fisal has some idea as to where we are.'

He understood what I was saying, and nodded vigorously, pointing an arm out straight.

'There.'

So, there was the way we went.

The ambush occurred around eleven that morning. It was now past five, and the sun was setting. The cool night air was closing in rapidly, making us pull our robes closer to our bodies.

'I wonder if we should make camp for the night, aunt. I've a little water and a few figs to eat. I don't think we should try and travel any further. Is Fisal leading us to an oasis or what?'

'A settlement called Beodab. It's right on the border, so hopefully we'll cross it and meet up with Cynthia and David. I'm sure we'll also hear news of Ackbar and the rest of the clan as well.'

According to Fisal, Beodab was another day's journey, so we made camp. We slept under the stars using a couple of rolled up carpets as cover after eating a supper consisting of a few figs and a little water.

I lay on my back, hands under my head, gazing up at the night sky. A myriad of twinkling stars gazed back at me. I even saw a couple streaking across the night sky.

The events of the day rushed through my mind like a runaway train.

How would all this end? Safely delivering the peacock, or having our lives cut short in this desolate place? I tried not to dwell on that thought.

Then oblivion.

FISAL TO THE RESCUE.

We awoke cold and stiff limbed. Even Fisal was subdued, his customary chattering strangely absent as we gathered our belongings together.

Molly and Prudence were persuaded to go down on their knees and we hoisted the luggage onto the saddles and strapped everything down tightly.

I felt pain in muscles I didn't even know I had. The way Matilda walked showed she felt the same.

I helped her mount Prudence, and once she was settled, Fisal scrambled up in front of her. It was obvious he was concerned about his family, and hoped he would hear news of them once we reached Beodab. They led the way with Molly and me bringing up the rear.

Once the warmth of the sun soaked into our aching bones, the painful stiffness in our bodies disappeared and along with it, our monosyllable conversation. Tongues loosened, and before long the three of us were chattering like magpies, going over the events of yesterday, and even able to raise a chuckle at what we must've looked like when the camels had taken fright and bolted.

We ambled on until midday, and then Fisal called a halt for a short break. We were so lucky to have him with us. We hadn't seen another soul all morning, so it was reassuring to have this child of the desert showing us the way. He knew exactly where he was taking us, or so it appeared. Our lives were literally in the hands of this slip of a boy.

A few sips of water were all he would allow, and then off we plodded again.

I noticed Matilda slumping in the saddle. Her chattiness of the morning had ceased, and I knew she was feeling the strain. By late afternoon she appeared exhausted, and I was getting worried.

'Are we close, Fisal?' I called out.

'Yes, yes, soon,' he replied.

'How soon?' I asked desperately.

'There' and he pointed ahead.

In the distance I could see smoke from campfires, and then makeshift buildings with tents scattered around.

It was Beodab.

Another fifteen minutes and we were riding into the settlement that had grown up around a small oasis. There was a semi-permanent feel about the place, and I found out afterwards it was a major halfway stop for restocking on provisions for camel caravans passing through to Ethiopia.

Fisal stopped Prudence outside a wooden one - storey building.

'Hotel,' he said.

I looked with some misgiving at this 'hotel.' I felt transported back to the old Wild West, except camels were tethered to the hitching posts instead of horses.

Disbelief must have shown on my face, because Fisal laughed and kept on saying, 'Yes, yes, hotel'

I jumped down off Molly and hurried to help Matilda.

'Soon have you in a nice soft bed, aunt,' I said to encourage her, as she leaned heavily on my arm.

'My bag?' she whispered.

'Don't worry, I've got it,' and helped her climb the few wooden steps into the hotel.

Fisal had gone on ahead to make arrangements, and we caught up with him bartering for a room. He was talking so fast, I couldn't make out one word of what he was saying, but he seemed satisfied with the result, going by the triumphant grin on his face.

I assisted Matilda to a bench near the door, and then helped Fisal bring in the luggage, which we carried to the room he'd arranged. He unlocked the door with the key the owner had given him, and I walked in, only to stop in dismay. There were no beds! In fact, there was no furniture at all. It was just a room.

Fisal read the look on my face and asked anxiously, 'Problem?'

Bless him. I quickly plastered a smile on my face and said, 'No, no Fisal. This is fine. We'll make up a comfy bed for Matilda, and then you can help me find some food, okay?'

'Food? Okay. No problem.'

I put a couple of the thin mattresses on top of each other, and with a little bit of improvisation, managed to make quite a decent bed.

At least we won't be bitten by bedbugs, as there are no beds, I thought with a wry smile.

I helped Matilda to the room, took off her heavy robe and headdress, and tucked her in snugly.

'Try and have a nap, aunt. I'm going with Fisal to get some food. The good thing about this room is it has a lock, so I'll lock the door on the way out. We won't be long. A good hot meal will see you right.'

'Be careful, Ella,' and Matilda squeezed my hand before drifting off to sleep.

I'd decided to keep my robe and headdress on, as I felt less conspicuous.

I gave Fisal money and told him to do all the talking.

We left the hotel and Fisal led me to another building, which I suppose one would call a shop, except it didn't have a counter or shelves. Tin goods were piled in boxes on the floor, bags of salt and flour on racks. Bulk buying was the order of the day. However, my helper haggled for a couple of tins of beef stew, sweet corn and tomatoes, as well as a packet of tea, sugar and three flat bread loaves.

With supper in hand, we made our way back to the hotel.

'I water camels and cook this,' said Fisal, and he disappeared.

I quietly unlocked the door to our room.

Matilda was sleeping soundly, so there was nothing to do but make myself as comfortable as possible and wait for Fisal to return.

He came back within the hour, carrying a large tray with plates full of heated up food, and three steaming mugs of tea. The aroma of the food permeated Matilda's unconsciousness, and she stirred.

'Is that supper I'm smelling?' and lifted herself up on one arm.

'Spot on, aunt. Come, let me help you.'

We ate in silence, this being our first decent meal in two days. By the time the last morsel of food and last swig of tea was swallowed, our spirits were considerably heightened.

Fisal was happy, as no bodies had been brought into Beodab, so he was confident his family were fine. Matilda's nap had recharged her batteries, and I was feeling relieved at the fact we were at the Ethiopian border without seeing any sign of our two nemesis.

Once supper was over, we decided on an early night and would make plans for carrying on our journey in the morning.

I had no inkling of the huge surprise in store as I settled myself in my makeshift bed, Fisal rolled up in a bundle at the foot of it.

Lying there waiting for sleep to steel over me, I couldn't help thinking how hard it was to believe that a body lying in Matilda's lounge could have started off a chain of events that would find us in a settlement in the desert, on the border of Ethiopia with a little boy of twelve our only means of security.

Madness!

What other adventures lay in store for us?

WHAT A SURPRISE!

Morning dawned, the early light peeping through gaps in the wooden shutters waking me from a restless sleep.

I stretched, and heard Matilda doing the same.

'Good morning, Ella. What a glorious sleep. I feel so refreshed; I could travel another hundred miles.'

'That's great, aunt,' and looked towards my feet.

'I wonder where Fisal is.'

No sooner were the words out of my mouth, and Fisal kicked open the door, bearing three mugs of tea and the remains of the bread from last night.

'Breakfast' he said, handing out the mugs, and then sat cross-legged on the floor.

'We leave today?' he asked Matilda.

'I do believe so, eh Ella?'

'If you really feel up to going, aunt. We'll check on the map to see exactly how far we are from Mega, and try and estimate how long it will take us.'

Fisal disappeared to get Molly and Prudence from their tethering posts, whilst Matilda and I packed up our belongings.

The camels were soon loaded, and we huddled over the map, trying to decide on the best route to follow.

We had to travel about hundred kilometres due east to reach Mega.

According to Fisal, the terrain was similar to what we'd been traveling through. He knew where the watering holes were, and thought we should reach Mega in three days. That would coincide with the arrival of Cynthia and David, therefore, optimism that our rendezvous would be successful, was high. Once again, we put our well-being in Fisal's capable hands.

He arranged extra water for us to take on the way, plus a substantial quantity of figs and other dried fruit. Bread was also packed; along with dried meat sticks that I hoped was not camel. Our remaining tea and sugar came along, plus more tins of stew, so food and water shouldn't be a problem.

I voiced my concern about passing through the border post, because I was sure Ken and co would have each one watched.

I was silly worrying about such mundane matters.

Fisal found border posts a joke, and assured us we would get into Ethiopia without a sniff of a border guard. Boring things such as passports and official entry stamps were totally immaterial to his people apparently.

Who was I to argue?

My other concern was Matilda and I were more conspicuous than we thought, even though we were wearing our robes. I felt, rather than saw, men glancing at us as we made our preparations. Two women traveling with just a little boy and no male companions was obviously causing some comment amongst the locals.

'I think the sooner we get out of here, the better, aunt. Have you noticed the funny looks we're getting?'

'It's because we have no male escorts Ella, although Fisal is doing a splendid job.'

'You have one now,' said a voice behind me.

I spun around, shock making my body go rigid.

I was staring at a very tall man, dressed in the local garb of loosely fitting robe and trousers with a turban wrapped around his head. But there was no mistaking the piercing black eyes and swarthy features of the mining commissioner.

'Jacob?'

'Jacob! Is that you under that turban? What a lovely surprise!' exclaimed Matilda. 'What on earth are you doing here, of all places?'

'I could be saying the same about you,' he replied, without taking his eyes off my face, or what he could see of it.

I was dumbfounded. This was a development I had not foreseen happening.

Fisal came bustling up.

'You have a problem with this man?' he asked Matilda.

'No, no Fisal. This is a good friend of ours. No problem at all.'

Fisal seemed satisfied with that explanation, and gently knocked Molly and Prudence on their forelegs to get them to kneel down so we could mount.

I climbed onto the saddle like an automaton.

Questions were rushing around my brain, the uppermost being, had we fallen into a trap?

As Prudence led the way, with Molly following her sister, I noticed Jacob get onto a camel, which a little boy had been holding for him. There were packed saddlebags and skin water containers firmly attached to the saddle. Jacob was well prepared for traveling in the desert, and going by the state of his clothes, it looked as though he'd done a fair bit before reaching us.

He pulled abreast of Molly and we rode in silence for a few moments whilst I desperately tried to think of something to say.

What came out of my mouth was pathetic.

'Well, Jacob. Fancy seeing you here.' (As I said, pathetic eh?')

Jacob paused a while before speaking.

'Are you going to tell me why you and Matilda are in Beodab, when you were supposed to be in England weeks ago?'

'Yes, of course I will. I'm sorry, Jacob. Meeting you like this took me totally by surprise. But let me ask you a question before I answer yours. What are you doing in the middle of the desert? Shouldn't you be on Tevrede?'

Jacob was having none of it.

'I'll explain why I'm here after you tell me why you changed your mind about going back to England.'

The ball was firmly back on my side of the court.

'Well' I said, choosing my words carefully. 'We met a delightful couple in Harare, traveling through Africa in a land rover. They needed a couple of passengers, so aunt and I jumped at the chance. I mean, what a lovely way of seeing more of the country before returning to England. There was no big hurry in getting back, anyway.'

Silence.

Then, 'Are you sure that's the only reason, Ella? Where are your companions now?'

'Oh, well, they had to make a detour on the way, but we're meeting up with them in a couple of days. Meanwhile, Matilda and I have been well looked after by our self-appointed guardian, Fisal. Travelling by camel has really been a lot of fun.'

I know what you're thinking.

I went from bad to worse. But it was the best I could do under the circumstances. I still had no idea where Jacob fitted into the scheme of things. If aunt hadn't found that scarf in his library, I probably would've taken him totally in my confidence, but she had, and it was an integral part of the puzzle.

'Anyway, Jacob. You still haven't told me how you come to be here.'

'To find you and your aunt,' he replied flatly.

Another silence.

He then continued.

'Believe me, it hasn't been easy. I first went to Harare and eventually found the hotel you'd stayed in. You conveniently left the postcard in your room, which the cleaners had handed to reception. It was put in a drawer and forgotten about until I asked questions about you. The receptionist was under the impression I was with the police as I bandied Stuart's name around, so she willingly told me what information she had. I was then sure you would make a stop in Nairobi.'

Jacob shook his head, obviously remembering something unpleasant.

He continued his narrative.

'So, I flew to Nairobi. Hotels are very reluctant to dish out information on their guests. But, I told the same story as I did in Harare and found out you left the hotel in the middle of the night, which obviously worried me.

It was relatively easy following your trail to Kalacha, but then events became confusing. I found the land rover had left with just a man and woman in it, but a camel caravan had departed on the same day. I could only think for some reason, you and Matilda had decided to travel along with it. Why you would want to do that I couldn't imagine.'

Jacob stopped talking, obviously expecting some sort of answer from me.

'We thought it would be fun,' I eventually said.

'Yes, well, fun or not, I followed the route you would've taken, on this camel, I might add, and then heard the news the camel train had been attacked by bandits. I eventually caught up with it at some oasis or other, and talked to the headman in charge. He called himself Ackbar and was very concerned for your safety.'

Before Jacob could say anymore, I called out to Fisal.

'Your grandfather is fine, Fisal. Hopefully, so is the rest of your family.'

He turned in the saddle, grinned and gave me the thumbs up.

'Sorry Jacob. You were saying?'

'I was saying Ackbar was very concerned about you and your aunt, and also his grandson. Fisal is his favourite, apparently. Anyway, I retraced my steps, and came to Beodab. I stopped for the night and was going to continue the search when I spotted you and your aunt. You do look conspicuous, even in the clothes you're wearing.'

'What about you?' I countered. 'Are you trying to pass yourself off as a local?'

'I thought I might blend into the scenery better. This area is notorious for its banditry.'

'Really,' I said. 'I would never have guessed.'

'Ella! You and Matilda have been incredibly fortunate to have got this far unmolested. What possessed you to do such a foolhardy thing is beyond me.'

That's where Jacob made his mistake.

Feelings of guilt had been increasing steadily whilst he'd been telling his story. That guilt was immediately replaced with indignation and anger at the censure in his voice.

How dare he criticize Matilda and me? Nobody asked him to scour Africa looking for us. We'd managed very well, as far as I was concerned.

'Okay Jacob,' I said tartly. 'You've found us. Now what?'

'I shall escort you to wherever you're going. It really isn't safe for two women and a young boy to be travelling unescorted in these parts.'

I then felt boorish.

The least I could do was to thank him for all the inconvenience and expense we'd put him through.

I didn't get very far.

'It's not your thanks I want, Ella,' Jacob interrupted. 'It's enough for me to know you and your aunt are safe,' and with that, Jacob urged his camel on to catch up with Matilda, leaving me feeling like a sulky schoolgirl.

Conflicting emotions surged through me; anger at his attitude, suspicious of his motives, but also, vexingly, heartfelt relief to have him near.

'Oh, blast you Jacob. Why didn't you stay on Tevrede where you belong,' I muttered under my breath.

The day wore on. The sun got hotter, a stiff wind began blowing, and I was getting heartily sick of this desert.

Molly must have felt my irritation, as she insisted on squabbling with her sister, nipping her on the legs and buttocks whenever she had the opportunity. Matilda got cross, as her ride on Prudence became more uncomfortable, until we all agreed it was time to call a halt for the day.

We'd stopped on a rise, which had a panoramic view of the surrounding area for about 180 degrees. Behind us was a cliff face rising steeply. At the bottom of the cliff was a cave Fisal and Jacob explored which proved to be absent of any wild animals that might have decided to make it their home.

We unpacked the camels, tethered them, and then made camp.

A fire was soon burning in the mouth of the cave, our mattresses invitingly laid out, and within half an hour, we were munching on beef stew, as well as fresh fruit Jacob had been carrying.

Matilda was in great spirits.

'It's lovely seeing Jacob again,' she'd said, as we laid our mattresses down on the smoothest bit of ground we could find. 'I must say I feel a lot safer now he's around. Imagine him going to all that trouble to find us. It must've been like looking for a needle in a haystack.'

'Yes, aunt. He did go through a lot of trouble tracking us down, but was it the peacock or us he was tracking? Be careful what you say. I still don't know if we can trust him or not.'

'Really, Ella! I do think you're over reacting to me finding that scarf in Jacob's library. He probably never even knew it was there in the first place.'

I didn't say anymore. Matilda had obviously made up her mind about Jacob, and only time would tell if she were right or not. Nothing I said was going to make any difference in her opinion of him.

I sat down by the campfire and Fisal handed me a cup of steaming tea.

Jacob joined me.

'Truce, Ella?' he asked with a rueful grin.

'Yes, of course, Jacob. I'm sorry about my earlier attitude. Put it down to being concerned about Matilda, and of course, knowing you were right, although it was ungentlemanly of you to say so.'

'I apologise. Worry can make a person say things without meaning to.'

And we both sat in silence, watching the flickering flames of the campfire, whilst sipping our mugs of tea.

After a while, the hot food loosened tongues, and Jacob told us stories of his upbringing in Zimbabwe, whilst Matilda, not to be outdone, recounted various adventures she'd had in her quest for treasures. She even brought up the one about the sheik wanting to buy me for a dozen camels, which made Jacob and Fisal go into fits of laughter.

'What do you think, Fisal?' asked Jacob, once he could speak again. 'Is she worth it?'

'No, no! Too thin!'

This started them both convulsing again.

I smiled at them tolerantly, and leant back against a rock, watching the shadows cast by the fire, flickering on the walls of the cave.

But as I looked, I noticed one shadow didn't seem to be acting the same as the others. It had a life of its own, and was creeping closer towards us.

I put out my hand and grasped Jacob around his wrist.

He turned and saw the alarm in my face.

I flicked my eyes towards the shadow.

Understanding dawned.

He put a finger to his lips, and glanced at Matilda and Fisal, who were unaware of anything happening, as Matilda was busy expanding Fisal's English vocabulary.

I saw Jacob's hand disappear underneath his sleeping bag and slowly withdraw, clutching his rifle.

The shadow was getting closer.

Matilda had stopped talking to Fisal and was looking at me with a frown on her face. I shook my head slightly at her, and began to talk about the weather, of all things, when Jacob suddenly leapt to his feet; rifle cocked, and sprinted around the side of the cave.

We heard scuffles in the darkness, a cry of pain, and then silence.

By this time, I was following the noises, and saw Jacob standing over the inert form of a man, dressed in local garb.

'Do you know him, Ella?'

I looked closely at his face. It wasn't easy to see in the shadows, but it did look familiar.

'I'm sure I've seen him before. Aunt! Does he look familiar to you?'

By this time, Matilda had scrambled over the rocks to see what was going on, Fisal bringing up the rear.

'Yes, I've seen him before, but where? Of course! It's the hotel owner from Beodab. But what's he doing skulking around here?'

'I would guess, following you and Ella. But why would he want to do that, I wonder?'

Matilda shook her head.

'I haven't a clue.'

'The obvious reason could be something to do with your attackers. Maybe this character has been paid to spy on you. When you were separated from the caravan, they could have left word at various places, that a reward would be paid to anyone who could track you down.'

He looked at the prostate figure lying at his feet.

'We'll tie him up, and when he regains consciousness, I'll ask him.'

Jacob was right.

Hassid had heard two men were looking for an elderly lady and her niece, and were willing to pay a good sum for information leading to their whereabouts. He'd been following us since we left Beodab, and was waiting for an opportunity to deal with Jacob. Murder was obviously on his mind, as he had a large scimitar he intended using, and then he was going to personally hand us over and claim his reward. Not a very pleasant person to know.

If Jacob hadn't turned up when he did, we would have been in an awful lot of trouble. But the fact Jacob had made the connection made me even more wary of his motives.

After reassuring us that everything would be fine, Jacob strode off to keep watch over Hassid, his rifle at the ready for any more unexpected visitors, whilst we tried to get some sleep.

Bandits!

The rest of the night passed uneventfully.

Another day and a half would see us in Mega.

We broke camp after breakfast, and our unwanted visitor was hoisted up onto the saddle of his camel, that Jacob found tethered a short distance away from the cave.

Fisal led us through totally unpopulated terrain. I didn't even know we had crossed the border until he twisted around in his saddle and called out, 'See! No border guards.'

'That's a relief,' I replied, and then wished I hadn't said anything, as I noticed Jacob giving me a hard stare.

I was about to try and explain my remark, but then thought better of it. As it happened, at that moment anyway, a cloud of dust drew my attention. The other members of the party also noticed it.

'Bandits!' yelled Fisal, and grabbed Prudence's reins from Matilda, dug his heels into the camel's side, and urged her behind some rocks. I did the same with Molly whilst Jacob brought up the rear, pulling the hotel owner behind him.

We quickly tethered the animals and crouched behind the rocks.

'How do you know they're bandits, Fisal? And if they are, shouldn't we try and out run them?'

This was from Matilda.

'They move too fast for camel train. Can only be bandits. Can only hide and hope they do not see us.'

We watched the cloud of dust get bigger.

Jacob retrieved his rifle and lay flat on his stomach, training the barrel on the approaching camels. As the dust cloud moved closer, I could make out at least a dozen animals, and what was disconcerting, the glint of rifles in the sun. The noise of the galloping camels on the rocky terrain was getting louder, but no louder than my heart, which was galloping in unison!

'They're coming straight for us,' said Jacob. 'Almost as though they know we're here.'

Then, without warning, Fisal suddenly jumped up, shimmied up a rock, and began shouting and waving his arms like crazy.

'No, Fisal! Get down. They'll see you,' and I scrambled after him.

Jacob beat me to it, but Fisal was like an eel and slipped out of his arms and ran towards the galloping camels.

'Grandfather! Grandfather!'

I looked at Matilda.

'Grandfather?'

'Good gracious, Ella. It's Ackbar!'

And so it was.

The panting camels came to a halt by the rocks we'd hidden behind.

The largest man in the party jumped down and lifted Fisal high in the air, before hugging him tightly. It was a very touching reunion between grandson and grandfather. Then Fisal's dad joined in, and I had a lump the size of the Rock of Gibraltar stuck in my throat.

Jacob, Matilda and I led our camels out into the open; the hotel owner still tied to his, and stood waiting, whilst Fisal was showered with hugs and kisses by the rest of his family.

Then Ackbar spotted us, and strode over.

'Miss Ella! Madam Matilda! It makes my heart feel very good to see you both standing there. Allah has answered my prayers and kept you from harm,' and he enveloped us in his massive arms.

'Along with a lot of help from Fisal,' I gasped, when I could breathe again. 'Your grandson is an amazing boy.'

'But of course!' replied Ackbar, spreading his arms out wide. 'He is my grandson.'

Enough said.

Ackbar turned to Jacob and held out his hand.

'Ha! Here is the knight in shining armour, as the English say,' and shook Jacob's hand vigorously. 'I am very pleased to meet again the friend of these two courageous ladies.'

There's no denying I felt a certain amount of satisfaction being called courageous, after Jacob had referred to us as foolhardy.

'My brother David and his wife are with the rest of the caravan and anxious to hear news of you.'

'Are you camped at Mega?'

'Yes. It is not far. If we hurry, we will get there early tomorrow morning. David was very concerned when he heard of the ambush at the gorge. He wanted to come and look for you, but I persuaded him to stay and fix his land rover.'

'Fix his land rover? Why? What's wrong with it?'

'A bullet through the radiator.'

'A bullet! So, their journey wasn't uneventful either. David and Cynthia are fine though, aren't they?'

'Yes! Yes! They are fine! Ha! That David. He enjoys the excitement very much, I think. And his wife! She worships him; therefore, everything he says and does is right. Even being shot at does not worry Madam Cynthia as long as her David is fine. What love!'

Ackbar then noticed the sullen gentleman sitting tied up on his camel.

'I know you,' said Ackbar. 'You are the thief that runs that hovel called a hotel in Beodab. Why is he with you people? And why is he tied up?'

Jacob gave a brief account of what had happened the previous night.

'We shall hand him over to the authorities when we get to Mega,' said Ackbar, and he mounted his camel and began to wax lyrical on the love there should be between a man and a woman. He was still quoting from the Karma Sutra, I think it was, when Matilda added her bit from Romeo and Juliet, and it wasn't long before a heated discussion sprang up between the two of them on who were the most famous lovers in history.

I left them to it, and pulled Molly back a little to ride alongside Jacob.

'Ackbar is quite a character, don't you think?'

'He certainly has yours and Matilda's interests at heart. How did you meet him?'

'Oh, he's a great friend of David. They've known each other for years.'

I paused for a moment, trying to pick my words carefully.

'You know, Jacob, now that we are close to the others, what are your plans? I'm feeling guilty at the time and expense we've put you through. I know how you must be longing to get back to Tevrede.'

'The farm is fine. Robert is keeping an eye on it. Let's get to Mega and decide there,' and Jacob turned the conversation to other more mundane topics. I had no option but to follow his lead.

The journey passed quickly.

Flanked on all sides by Fisal's relatives, Molly and Prudence seemed spurred on by the presence of the other camels. We made such good time Ackbar decided to push on to Mega instead of making camp for the night.

At nine that evening, we could see lights shining in the distance. Mega at last.

Ackbar led us to his tent, and we dismounted, Jacob giving Matilda a helping hand.

'Ella! Matilda! What a relief to see you both,' and there was David and Cynthia arms outstretched ready to give us a welcome hug.

How great it was to see them.

Punch and Judy.

We were sitting around the campfire.

Our story of the journey through the desert, ambush at the gorge, and subsequent events had been told, including meeting Jacob and our unexpected visitor in the cave.

Now it was David and Cynthia's turn.

David narrated.

'After we left you with Ackbar, we drove towards Moyale, which, as you know, is a border post. We didn't push it, knowing that it was going to take you at least two weeks to get to Mega, so we took in a bit of sight-seeing along the way. There are the most amazing villages hewn out of cliff faces, and people live in them. Absolutely stunning! Anyway, after spending ten days on the road without any problems at all, we reached Moyale. That's where we met up with your assailants, plus a woman with them.'

'A woman! What did she look like?'

'She had a mop of frizzy yellow hair, and the longest chin I've ever seen.'

'Stephanie! My goodness Ella, that sounds just like Stephanie Stone from Swingen Linen. That proves Ken and co are working for her.'

'Who's Stephanie Stone, Matilda?'

'Somebody I met in England about a year ago. We were wondering if she's involved in all that's been happening.'

I quickly jumped into the conversation, as I was worried Matilda had forgotten Jacob knew little, if anything, about that side of things. He was sitting beside me listening intently.

'So, David, what happened next?'

'Well, we did try and sidle into town without being too obvious, but we must've been noticed, although they never made their move until later. Remember I said we were going to report the helicopter attack when we reached Kalacha Dida? We did just that, so I think they were reluctant to approach us in town. It's possible they'd been questioned about the affair.'

'What helicopter attack?' asked Jacob.

'Didn't Ella tell you we were fired on from a helicopter?'

'No, she didn't,' he replied, looking at me.

I shrugged but kept quiet.

'Anyway,' David continued, 'we decided to spend the night at Moyale, and slowly make our way here the next day. We had just over three days in hand before our appointed time to meet you. Everything went fine until we were about fifty miles outside of Moyale, when that damn helicopter buzzed us again. I decided not to try and make a run for it, but to carry on driving sedately until it made its move. Remember, Ella, we were going to give them a nonsense story about which way you and Matilda went. Well, they followed us for about ten miles and then pulled away and disappeared. Great, we thought. They are well and truly flummoxed. No Ella. No Matilda. They realise they're on a wild goose chase.'

David paused dramatically in his narrative.

'We were totally wrong!'

'Why? What happened?' asked Matilda.

'We were kidnapped.'

'What!'

This was worse than I thought.

'Yes, Ella. It was very exciting.'

This from Cynthia who decided to add her bit.

'That evening, we camped by a small village near a river, and as we were eating supper, out from the bushes came your two friends, plus the helicopter pilot and the frizzy haired woman.'

Cynthia stopped talking, and smiled at her husband.

'They were very angry with us David, weren't they? The pilot was not happy at being shot at.'

'He's even angrier now.'

'Why? What did you do?' asked Matilda.

'I'll come to that in a minute,' David answered with a grin, and continued telling us how they were forced at gunpoint to pack everything in the land rover, and how Ken drove with them, keeping his gun pointed at the back of David's head.

'We eventually stopped at a small airfield, and drove into a hanger. The other three followed us in their car. The chopper was inside the hanger. Once we stopped, Ken waved his gun at us, demanding to know where you were. We feigned total ignorance, and told them we'd dropped you off somewhere in the desert, as you insisted on not driving with us anymore. Eventually, the woman told him to stop, and being held captive with the threat of death hanging over us, might sway us into revealing what we knew. I said the usual things about not knowing what they were talking about, and how they'll never get away with it etc. Eventually they got fed up with us, and we were locked in a store room until they made up their minds what to do next.'

David paused for a moment.

'Oh, you poor dears!' exclaimed Matilda. 'What a terrible ordeal.'

'It was fine, Matilda,' said Cynthia. 'David knew he would find a way for us to escape, but he wanted to learn more about these people first, didn't you David?'

'Well, I could see the woman was in charge, as the others took orders from her. The private airfield and helicopter were obviously at her disposal, and you could tell she was used to calling the shots. So, I hoped to find out more before we left.'

'And did you?' asked Matilda.

'Oh yes. Plenty. But I'll come to that later.'

David then spoke about being locked in a storeroom and hearing a car leaving the hanger.

'This was one time I was glad of my lanky frame. The only window in the room was a small skylight above the door. It was easy for me to stretch and look out of it, in time to see the woman, plus Ken and co drive away, leaving the pilot to guard us.'

David stopped talking for a moment, obviously savouring the memory of what happened next.

'You escaped?' I asked, impatient to know more.

'Yes. When I looked out of the window, I could see the top of the man's head. He was standing right in front of the door. Silly place to stand. All I had to do was take a few running steps and kick the door down. It flattened the pilot, knocked him out cold. We tied him up, put a gag in his mouth, and sat him in his seat in the helicopter. I whipped out the plug wires, and for good measure, cut the transmission belt. We wanted to make sure that chopper wasn't going to take off in a hurry.'

Cynthia took up the narrative.

'We hurried to the office we'd noticed when driving into the hanger. There were crates and boxes piled around the walls. We opened a few, and the contents will interest you considerably, Matilda. We've brought along a few samples, plus some papers out of the filing cabinet. We then decided we'd outstayed our welcome, and David took out the spare key he always keeps in his sock, and we drove off in the land rover.'

'It seems to me our friends totally underestimated you two,' said Matilda, with a chuckle. 'I wonder why they didn't tie you up before locking the store room door.'

'They did,' said Cynthia, 'but David always keeps his penknife in his socks as well as the spare key. Cutting the cords didn't take long,' and she looked admiringly at her husband, as well she might.

Jacob finally joined in the conversation.

'What happened next?'

'We had the impression they were a bit panicky. That's probably why our kidnapping and subsequent imprisonment was really rather amateurish. Our impression was correct. I drove out of the hanger and headed for some undergrowth on the other side of the runway and switched off the engine. The land rover was well hidden. I thought we'd wait a while, as it was still several hours before sunrise, and see what developed. I was pretty sure that once our escape was discovered, our friends would think we'd taken off as fast as possible.'

David looked at his wife and grinned.

'We didn't have long to wait, did we Cynthia? Ten minutes later the three of them returned. They were furious at finding us gone, but what was interesting, was the reaction of the woman. She kept on shouting, 'We must find them before Stuart knows they're gone.'

I felt Jacob go rigid beside me.

Matilda gasped, and was about to say something, but quickly closed her mouth when she saw the warning look I gave her.

'Go on David.' I said.

'Not much more to tell. They obviously found the pilot, then realised the helicopter was out of commission, so, after locking the hanger, they all piled into their car with the woman still shouting about the dire things Stuart, whoever he is, would do to them if we weren't found.'

'And the bullet hole in the radiator?' I asked.

'That happened close to Mega. They ambushed us on the outskirts, but before then, I'd managed to get a message to Ackbar, saying we needed help, as I was sure they'd guess where we were heading, and probably some sort of reception would be waiting for us. Ackbar and his family organised their own reception committee, so Ken and co only managed to get off a few shots before they were scared away by Ackbar's gun touting family. We arrived yesterday, and have been well guarded ever since.'

We sat in silence attempting to mentally digest all that David and Cynthia had told us.

Matilda broke the reverie.

'All I can say is thank goodness you two escaped unharmed. If we'd known all this was going to happen, we would never have involved you.'

'Are you kidding, Matilda! All my other trips through Africa have been really boring compared to this one. It's been great fun, hasn't it Cynthia?'

She smiled her beautiful smile and nodded.

I looked at these two in amazement. Did nothing faze them?

'Well everybody,' said Matilda. 'I don't know about you, but I'm very tired, so I'm saying goodnight. If you don't mind, David, I'll look at whatever it is you found in the morning.'

That signalled the break-up of the campfire.

Goodnights echoed in the darkness as we made our way to our tents.

Jacob escorted us.

'Good night Jacob,' said Matilda, and she disappeared inside.

'Good night Matilda,' answered Jacob, then, as I turned to follow aunt, Jacob put his hands on my shoulders and looked intently into my face.

'I know you're keeping a lot of things from me, Ella. I have no idea why you seem to find it so hard to trust me, but I hope the time will come when you do,' and after dropping a light kiss on my brow, abruptly turned and strode off into the darkness.

I entered the tent to find Matilda sitting up in bed, waiting impatiently for me.

'Good, you're here. What do you make of it Ella? Could Stuart be our inspector, or is it just a huge coincidence?'

I collapsed on my mattress. I have to admit the events of the day had taken their toll.

'I don't know, aunt. When David mentioned the name Stuart, Jacob definitely showed some reaction, but whether that means anything I haven't a clue. Maybe when we see whatever it is David and Cynthia took from the office, we'll have a better idea. Meanwhile, let's sleep on it, and be thankful they're fine. I shudder to think what could have happened to them. We both know how ruthless Ken and co can be.'

'You're right, my dear. Shame, you look as though you could fall asleep standing up.'

I didn't quite do that, but it was a close thing.

STOLEN TREASURE.

The next morning found us peering at the samples David and Cynthia had purloined.

'My goodness me!' exclaimed Matilda. 'I recognize this,' and she held up a figure six inches high, carved out of green stone.

'This piece is from the Ming dynasty, and was stolen from a private collection of Ming porcelain and jade pieces that was on show at the Ottawa Museum in Canada. This particular piece was the most valuable. In fact, it's priceless, because it's one of a kind. The authorities always thought whoever stole it, knew exactly what they were after, because nothing else was taken.'

'When did this happen, aunt?'

'About six months ago. The owner insisted on absolute confidentiality as she thought if there was any reporting of the theft, who ever took it would go underground so to speak and the piece would never see the light of day again. The trail of the jade was tracked to Rotterdam, then nothing.'

'What about this piece?' and Cynthia held up a bracelet that I thought looked pretty ordinary, but according to Matilda, adorned the wrist of a Viking princess aeons ago.

'That piece was also stolen from a private collection, although it was showing in London at the time. Did all the crates and boxes have stolen treasures like this, David?'

'Not exactly. When we opened a crate, it was full of rolls of material, but hidden in the folds were these items. I suppose we can assume more were hidden. The origin of the material was African, so it looks like a legitimate business was hiding a profitable illegitimate business, smuggling stolen treasure.'

'And the papers?' asked Matilda.

'Import and export manifestos with the name Swingen Linen as the company, exporting ethnic materials to different warehouses around Europe. A few priceless treasures tucked amongst the folds, more than pays import tax.'

This confirmed our suspicions that Swingen Linen was involved. The problem though, was what to do with the information we had.

Obviously, the authorities had to be told, but equally obviously, now that Swingen Linen had been exposed for what it was, how to go about catching them before they all did a disappearing act.

Surely the operation at the airfield had been wrapped up quickly once it was discovered artefacts and manifestos had been taken. Would our friends still pursue the peacock? Would they be even more determined to silence us, or would they cut their losses and head for the nearest rock to crawl under? Should we take Jacob into our confidence, or did his friendship with Inspector Stuart keep him on the suspect list?

What a dilemma!

And on that thought, Jacob strode into the tent.

A long silence ensued, broken by Cynthia speaking in her gentle voice.

'I really think it's time Jacob knew what was going on, Ella. I know you've told us about your fears of who this Stuart could be, but I really think you should give Jacob the benefit of the doubt.'

David and Matilda nodded in agreement.

I looked at each one in turn, and then looked at Jacob. His face was expressionless. No way was he going to make this easy for me.

I made up my mind.

'Jacob, let's take a stroll together,' and I hooked my arm into his, and we walked out of the tent.

Neither of us said anything until we'd wandered a little distance from the tents and perched ourselves on some rocks under the shade of a cluster of palm trees.

I did notice a couple of Ackbar's relatives, rifles resting snugly in their arms; settle themselves a little distance away from us.

Now we've got our own bodyguards.

Jacob sat in silence, waiting for me to begin.

So, I told him about Matilda and I finding the two scarves, the fax and printout and then Matilda making the discovery of the third scarf in a book in his library, and how we put the three together to make one whole. I told him about Tevrede being lost in a poker game all those years ago, and finding the peacock, and our decision to take it to Ethiopia ourselves. I mentioned my distrust of Inspector Stuart, especially when we saw Ken and co roaming freely in Harare, and how I felt Jacob was guilty by association, knowing the inspector was a friend of his.

Jacob listened impassively until I reached this bit.

'Ella! If only you'd spoken to me before now, I would have warned you about the inspector.'

'What! What do you mean?'

'I was uneasy about the way Charles was investigating your case. The morning you left Tevrede, I heard him on the phone in the library. The door was slightly open, and I was just about to push it wider, when I heard him mention your name. It was what he said about you that made me really worried.'

Jacob stopped talking. I glanced at him, only to see him shaking with silent laughter.

'Okay. You've had your fun. What did the inspector say about me?'

'That you were a flaming nuisance, and then he began reprimanding whoever was on the other end of the line, telling them not to mess up again, but to get the parcel and finish the job properly.'

Jacob paused.

'Go on.' I was impatient to hear the rest of his story.

'His words could've been taken two ways. Firstly, that you were hampering his investigations, or secondly, he was somehow involved in the whole business himself. I began to think the latter because he tried to get me to tell him where you were staying in Harare, and when you were flying to England. I couldn't tell him because I didn't know.

I'd noticed during dinner on our last evening, neither you nor Matilda elaborated on your travel plans. I thought that might've been solely for my benefit, but looking back, I can see you were worrying about Charles even then.'

'Yes we were, and for good reason. I'm sure we would never have made it to England if we'd followed our original plans.'

I then asked Jacob why he went to so much trouble looking for us.

'The more I thought about how you left Tevrede so abruptly, and remembering Charles's phone call, and then finding out he'd called off the search for your attackers the day after you left, the more worried I was about your safety.'

'He called off the search?' I exclaimed. 'I was right about that then.'

'I found out about it when a police officer from Gweru came to the farm with a telegram for Charles. By that time, he'd already left for England, or so I thought. I decided to open it. It read, 'Confirmation of message. Search terminated.' That's all it said. There was no clue as to who'd sent it, but by then, I was putting two and two together and making a decided four.

So, I decided to look for you. I wanted to get hold of Charles and ring his neck, but I was worried about tipping him off with what I already knew, thereby putting you and Matilda in more danger. The rest you know.'

Jacob stopped talking, waiting for my response.

I gazed across the desert. I still had some unanswered questions.

'So, I wasn't wrong when I felt you react when Inspector Stuart's name was mentioned last night?'

'Everything began to fall into place.'

'And the scarf? What about the scarf found in your library?'

'I have no idea where that scarf came from. You must believe me, Ella. The scarf and hearing Tevrede was lost in a poker game!'

Jacob shook his head, obviously perplexed.

So, there were still two mysteries to be solved.

'I wonder,' said Jacob, staring into the distance, frowning, making his infamous eyebrows even more satyr looking.

'You wonder what?'

'Remember I mentioned my father was dead, the first evening you were at Tevrede?'

'Yes, I do. I deliberately didn't ask you any questions, because you seemed reluctant to talk about it.'

'I was. The thing is he was murdered, although the police said it was an accidental death. I never believed it at the time, and still don't.'

'Oh no, Jacob. I'm so very sorry. Why do you think it was murder?'

'I found my father close to the hill that's behind the farmhouse. His neck was broken. The police said his horse must've bolted after being startled by a snake, and threw him. That explanation just doesn't make sense.'

'Why?'

'Because I found him amongst the thorn trees that grow in that area. My father would never have taken a horse into those trees. It would have been ripped to pieces. No, he was on foot for some reason. I could never understand why he was in that area in the first place.'

'Maybe he was looking for the mine entrance. Matilda and I used machetes to hack our way through.'

Jacob looked at me, conflicting emotions flashing across his face.

'The thing is Charles Stuart was staying with us at the time, so he conducted the investigation. He was the one who insisted my father must've fallen off his horse and broke his neck. My mother never got over dad's death. She knew what a good rider he was, but I just couldn't prove otherwise. Now I might have a chance.'

'I wonder if your father came across the scarf and hid it in the book, but died before he had a chance to tell you about it. But how did the inspector come to be staying at your farm?'

'Stuart came to the mining office and told me he was on secondment with the Gweru police and needed a place to stay. Could I recommend a hotel? It seems so obvious now what he was up to, as there's the Meikles Hotel just down the road! Obviously, I invited him to stay with us. I think he was counting on that. As you know we have plenty of spare rooms. It would have been churlish not to offer. It's possible he tracked the scarf to Tevrede and had to silence my father, who somehow had it in his possession, and had connected it to the mine, but didn't really know what he was looking for.'

Jacob sat quietly, obviously lost in thought. I kept quiet, waiting for him to continue.

Eventually he said, 'I would like to see the map and papers showing Tevrede lost in a poker game. I have no idea whether that would stand up in court after all this time, or not.'

'Well, both Philip and his uncle are dead; so we'll never know if they were after the farm or the peacock, or both.'

I looked at Jacob and smiled.

I must admit I was feeling more cheerful than I was first thing this morning. I was confident Jacob was telling the truth. We knew for sure Inspector Stuart was involved, and how satisfying it would be to have the death of Jacob's father finally explained and the murderer caught. Obviously, Inspector Stuart was the prime suspect.

'I'm glad we've had this talk. It will make things much easier now I know I can trust you.'

Jacob turned to face me.

'I have something to say to you, Ella that I haven't said to any other person and that is, I love you. No, I don't want you to say anything. I understand you hardly know me, but I hope to rectify that in the future. When you walked into the mining office with Matilda, I knew you were the one. It's as simple as that.

Now, I realize this is not the time or place to discuss my personal feelings for you, especially under the watchful eye of our two chaperones, so let's go back to the others. We have some planning to do. Once this saga is over, I hope to resume where I left off,' and Jacob pulled me to my feet, keeping hold of my hand as we walked back to David and Cynthia's tent.

Matilda saw us coming.

'Everything sorted out, Ella?' she asked, as we got closer.

'Yes, I believe so.'

'Good girl.'

THE ADVENTURE CONTINUES.

I think you would agree when I say the five of us were way out of our league in this situation.

An international smuggling operation, a top ranking policeman, so bent, his nose was touching the ground, several heavies whose hobby was murder, and a witch, made up the scenario we found ourselves in, the peacock being the prize for the winner.

Matilda was still hell bent on getting the peacock to Addis Ababa; Jacob just wanted aunt and I safely ensconced at Tevrede until everything was sorted out; David wanted to get Interpol involved; and Cynthia, well, Cynthia just wanted whatever David wanted.

I refused point blank to be wrapped up in cotton wool, which caused those notorious eyebrows of Jacob to take on that satyr look again. We were arguing over this point, when Matilda raised her hands and said, 'Come, come children! Let's not argue. Jacob! It's obvious Ella will not allow herself to be bundled off back to Tevrede after we've come so close to our ultimate destination. She feels as strongly as I do about handing the peacock over to the museum, and to have come this far and just give up? No! I can understand my niece being obstinate as a mule, as you so delicately put it.

David is right saying we must contact the authorities, but we can do that when we get to Addis Ababa. We're so close, and if we contact the police now, they'll take away the peacock, and it could be months or years even before it's finally handed over to the Ethiopians, if ever. You know how long winded we British can be over red tape. After all, we invented the stuff.'

'What do you say, David?' asked Jacob. 'Shall we help the ladies get this peacock to where it has to go, or shall we contact the police and have done with it?'

David looked at Matilda.

Who could resist that pleading look in her eyes? No one, least of all our gentle giant.

'Addis Ababa here we come, and once the peacock is safely delivered, we contact Interpol and wash our hands of Ken and co, Stuart, Swingen Linen and that Stephanie woman.'

Who can you trust?

Ackbar was sorry to see us leave the next morning, but we felt he'd done far more than was expected of him. To put the clan in even more danger was not an option.

Fisal was devastated.

'Come, little man,' said Matilda. 'One day you must visit England for a long holiday. You can stay with me in my cottage, and I will show you all the beautiful places England has. Will that be alright with you Ackbar?'

'But of course,' he boomed, and lifted the now grinning Fisal onto his shoulders.

We clambered aboard the land rover and the whole clan waved us off, broadcasting the fact to all and sundry.

'That was quite a send-off,' I remarked to Matilda. 'Ken is bound to have someone watching the camp. He's sure to know we've left.'

And that is exactly what we want him to think.

'Hold on everybody,' called out David from the front. 'We have exactly fifteen minutes to get to the pick-up point,' and then put foot to the peddle, causing us to shoot forward.

'Anybody following?' he called after ten minutes.

'Not that I can see,' answered Jacob, swivelling around to look out the back window.

Five minutes later, David swerved violently to the right, and went crashing through the bush. We hung on tightly to the hand straps, as we bumped along a barely discernible track.

Suddenly, we were in a clearing, and David screeched to a halt.

'One minute to spare,' and as he said those words, the sound of a light aircraft could be heard.

'He's just coming in to land. Quick Ella, Matilda! Out you get,' and we scrambled out of the land rover, Matilda clutching her carpetbag.

We ran to the now waiting plane, and the pilot hustled us on board.

Once seated, I looked out of the window to see the land rover already racing back down the track to the road.

'You are comfortable?' bellowed the pilot, who just happened to be one of Ackbar's many cousins.

I grinned and nodded my head.

Abdul gave us each a pair of headphones, and once we had adjusted them, he said through the earpiece, 'we shall be landing in Addis Ababa within the hour. Please enjoy the trip,' and once settled back in his cockpit, gave us the most nerve wracking flight I have ever been on.

I have to admit I spent most of it with my eyes tightly closed, as Abdul obviously enjoyed the thrill of flying as low as possible, skimming the tops of trees whilst taking the shortest route to the capital.

We came in to land at Addis Ababa airport.

I looked at Matilda. She'd loved every minute of the flight, and eyes sparkling with excitement said, 'Almost there Ella. We've nearly done it.'

'So we have, aunt.'

We landed, and no sooner did we have our feet on terra firma, we were whisked off to a waiting helicopter Abdul had arranged.

'In you go,' and I was bodily lifted and deposited into the cockpit, followed by Matilda, her carpetbag still glued to her body.

Abdul gave the thumbs up sign to the helicopter pilot, closed the door and we took off, veering steeply to the left, and then soaring above the airport buildings.

The pilot never said a word.

I felt my stomach do a flip flop, and we made a rapid descent towards a building surrounded on all sides by lush green lawns, thirstily soaking up shimmering sprays of water supplied by dozens of sprinklers. Swaying palm trees and sparkling fountains completed the picture.

This must be it, and I nudged Matilda and pointed. She nodded in agreement.

Soon the helicopter was hovering about two feet off the roof.

I jumped out first, and then helped Matilda down.

The pilot waved and flew off.

We looked around to get our bearings.

Three-foot high stone walls surrounded the perimeter of the flat sun bleached roof, and to the left, a small building and door allowing access to the interior.

'I hope to goodness it isn't locked,' and held my breath as I turned the handle.

Phew! Relief.

The door opened onto a staircase, which wound its way down the inside wall of the museum.

We clattered down the stone staircase until we came to a door that had a large 4 written on the lintel. We opened the door to find ourselves in a huge room filled with display cabinets containing pottery of all different shapes and sizes.

'Goodness, Ella! Look at this. I've never seen a finer specimen of an olive oil container of the Byzantine era than this.'

'That's great, aunt, but we have to find Mr. Hassan, the curator.'

'Yes, of course. We can always come back later to browse,' and Matilda regretfully pulled her eyes away from the urn.

'There's someone sitting by that door over there. It looks like a guide. I'm sure he'll know where Mr Hassan is,' and hurried over to ask him.

The guard was absorbed reading a newspaper, so he got quite a fright when Matilda tapped him on his shoulder and said, 'Excuse me!' in her school marm voice.

He looked at aunt, then me, then back to aunt again.

Going by the puzzled expression on his face, he was obviously trying to work out how we'd suddenly appeared without passing him to get into the room.

'Good morning. My name is Matilda Syndham and this is my niece Dr Ella Stanbridge. We are both archaeologists. Please be so kind as to take us to the curator Mr Hassan,' said aunt slowly and distinctly.

'Mr Hassan? I am terribly sorry; Mr Hassan is away for two days. He will return on Thursday.'

The Oxford accent, plus the news the curator was not at the museum was something we hadn't anticipated. We looked blankly at one another.

'However,' the guide continued, 'Mr Ishmael is standing in for Mr Hassan until he returns.'

'That's a relief,' replied aunt. 'Please can you take us to him?'

'Certainly. Follow me.'

We followed the guide down two flights of stairs and walked along a passage until we came to an office with Museum Curator stencilled on the door.

The guard knocked, waited a few seconds, then opened the door and disappeared inside, closing it behind him. After a minute, the door opened and the guide waved us into the office.

He stood back to let us enter, and then quietly closed the door behind him.

We were in a room that resembled an untidy warehouse, rather than an office. It was crowded with open and unopened boxes and crates full of every conceivable article ranging from pottery, books, jewellery, basket work, copper curios, fossils, bits and pieces of ceramics, the list was endless.

In the midst of it all, sitting at an oval desk, that was itself covered in bric a brac, was a very rotund gentleman, wearing a pair of pince nez on the end of a large, bulbous nose, which kept twitching as the tassel from his fez tickled it. A pair of tiny black eyes looked over the edge of his glasses, as we carefully made our way to the middle of the room.

Putting two podgy hands adorned in gold rings down on the desk to lever his girth to an upright position, he slowly rose to greet us.

His moon shaped face became even rounder as his full pink lips parted in a grimace that presumably was supposed to be a smile.

He shook our hands.

It was like clasping a pound of lard that was in the process of melting. My hand disappeared, only to reappear feeling squashed and slimy.

If I'm giving the impression I didn't like Mr Ishmael, you're right.

I glanced at Matilda.

The look on her face was reminiscent of a mouse confronting a snake.

'Please, my dear ladies. Let me find you chairs,' and Mr Ishmael bustled his bulk around the desk to pull up two chairs hiding behind a couple of crates.

Once we were settled, he went back to his desk, put his podgy hands together, rested his double chin on the tips of his fingers, and said, 'It is a pleasure having such a well-known person in the archaeological world condescending to visit our little museum, Mrs. Syndham. Are you here for any particular reason, or have you just dropped in for a visit?'

Was it my imagination, or did he emphasize the words, 'dropped in?'

Warning bells clanged in my head. How would he know of aunt and her hobby? Was she that famous?

'We were passing through Addis Ababa and I said to my niece we couldn't possibly spend time in the city and not visit the world-renowned museum. I was hoping you might be so kind as to show us any interesting artefacts you might have that would make our visit really worthwhile,' gushed Matilda. 'I know you have some remarkable exhibits from the Byzantine era which are the envy of every museum in the world.'

'Yes, yes we do, although one hesitates to boast, but yes indeed, the Byzantine era is very well represented here. If you ladies wouldn't mind waiting, I will summon Isaac, the guide who brought you to the office. He is well versed in that age of history. His conducted tours are extremely informative. I'm sure you will not be disappointed in what he has to show you. I would have been honoured to have conducted you myself, but, as you can see,' and he waved his fat loathsome hands above the clutter on his desk, 'I am unfortunately very busy cataloguing these latest finds, which have to be done before Mr. Hassan returns from his trip into the interior.'

As Mr. Ishmael was speaking, he was manoeuvring himself pass all the paraphernalia cluttering the office, until he came to the door.

'Just wait here a moment. I shall be back shortly,' and he opened the door and disappeared.

As soon as he left, I shot out of my chair.

'Aunt, we must get out of here quickly.'

'Let's go,' and Matilda gripped her carpetbag and legged it to the door.

Of course, we were too late.

As she went to grab the door handle, it turned, and there we were, face to face with Ken.

'Oh, damn and blast it,' she muttered, stepping back.

I was just behind her.

A quick glance around the office showed there was only one way in and one way out, and Ken was blocking it, with Mr. Ishmael bringing up the rear.

As Ken walked into the office, aunt and I slowly backed away, until our backs were up against some wooden crates. I had my hands behind me, searching for a specific item I'd seen and thought might come in handy.

Wooden crates need crowbars to pries the lids loose. My fingers felt the comforting coolness of metal, and I grasped it.

Ken wasn't paying any attention to me at all. His eyes were fixed on Matilda's carpetbag.

He reached for it. Aunt jerked the bag away.

I lifted the crowbar high in the air, and came down as hard as I could on his arm. I had no idea breaking bone would sound like the crack of a gunshot. That noise was immediately replaced by a piercing scream. Ken collapsed on the floor, whimpering, clutching his shattered arm to his chest.

Matilda swung the carpetbag and hit the shocked Mr. Ishmael on the side of his head, causing his fez to go flying through the air and the rest of him to be knocked sideways away from the door.

We shot out of the office and raced towards the stairs. I grabbed the carpetbag from Matilda, and hooked my arm into hers to help her along. Visitors to the museum stopped and looked at us curiously as we clattered down the marble stairs to the ground floor and headed for two large glass doors which I hoped was the entrance to the museum.

I could hear running footsteps behind us.

'Stop those ladies! They are thieves!' yelled Mr. Ishmael.

Hands reached out to grab us, but fear gave us the strength we needed to brush them aside as though they were twigs.

We burst through the glass doors and ran down the flight of steps leading up to the entrance.

'Which way, Ella?' panted Matilda.

A long expanse of lawn greeted us. No chance of running across that grass without being caught.

Then I noticed a minibus parked under the shade of a palm tree. The driver had obviously dropped off tourists wanting to visit the museum. He was now standing a little way from the vehicle, chatting to some cronies, drinking a cool drink.

'Come aunt. Let's hope the keys are in the ignition,' and I grabbed Matilda's arm and hurried towards the bus.

Our luck was in. The keys dangled invitingly.

Before the driver could grasp what was happening, the engine roared to life, and we were racing down the drive. In the rear view mirror, I could see Mr. Ishmael and Isaac standing at the top of the steps staring at us. There was no sign of Ken, which didn't surprise me.

'They won't be standing like that for long. We must lose ourselves and ditch this minibus as quickly as possible. Then we have to try and reach the others before they make their way to the museum.'

I glanced quickly at Matilda. Apart from being short of breath, she didn't look too bad.

'My word, Ella. Is there nobody we can trust?' she muttered bitterly. 'The world's made up of crooks!'

'Yes, well, you can add us to that number. Assault, battery and vehicle theft will look good on our charge sheets.'

We screeched to a halt at the end of the driveway, and then merged into the traffic. At the first opportunity I shot up a side street, then another and another. I had absolutely no idea where I was going. My overriding thought was to get far away from the museum that had nearly become our trap.

'Is anyone following us aunt?'

Matilda had been twisting in her seat, peering out the back window.

'Not that I can see, although, is that police sirens I can hear?'

'Quite likely. Ken has probably convinced the police we've stolen the peacock from the museum. We have to ditch this minibus, but where?'

'In that parking lot over there,' said Matilda, pointing her finger to the left.

'Perfect. There are so many minibuses parked, they'll have a hard job identifying this one,' and I squeezed the vehicle between two almost identical ones.

'What is this place anyway?'

'Looks like a sport stadium. Maybe there's a football match on. That's why there are so many buses.'

'Check in the cubby-hole for a map, aunt. Seeing as this is a tourist bus, it's quite possible the driver has a map of Addis Ababa tucked away. If we can pinpoint where this stadium is, we should be able to figure out how to get to the others before they land themselves in trouble.'

'Got it. I'll leave some money to cover the cost.'

'Right. Let's see if we can find the name of this stadium. There should be a sign close to the entrance.'

I locked the minibus and slipped the keys through a small hole in one of the side windows.

We made our way through the car park to the entrance. In huge gold lettering, first in Ethiopian, then in English, was the name Hail Sallasi.

'That should be easy to find on the map,' and Matilda smoothed it out between us on a wooden bench in the shade of the stadium.

We actually found the museum first.

I tried retracing our steps as well as I could remember, considering our flight was done in panic mode. The stadium was close to the main railway station.

'Let's see where the other three are entering Addis Ababa,' and I found the main road they were taking that led to the museum. After checking the time on Matilda's watch, I realised the rendezvous time was in an hour.

'It's now 1pm. We arranged to meet the others at the museum entrance at 2pm. We have to stop them going there. If my calculations are correct, we're actually only about three miles from the museum. We should be able to find a taxi to take us there.'

I thought back to the morning's events, one in particular standing out in my mind.

'Ken is probably at a hospital getting his arm fixed.'

I shuddered, remembering the sound of his arm breaking.

'Try not to think about it, Ella. You had no choice but to do what you did. He didn't have second thoughts about trying to kill us.'

'I know, aunt. But that doesn't make me feel any better. Anyway, let's see where we can get hold of a taxi. There should be plenty around.'

And there was, waiting for the stadium to empty.

I showed the driver where we wanted to go on the map.

'No problem.'

We clambered in, the carpetbag tucked between us.

'I wonder where Ken's cohort has been hiding. Not like him not to be around,' remarked Matilda.

'Yes, it does seem strange. However, let's concentrate on the problems at hand, and hope he doesn't show up.'

I looked out of the taxi window. Buildings, vehicles and pedestrians whizzed past.

'At this rate, we shall be at the rendezvous point in plenty of time.'

'The museum is soon,' said our driver, and he screeched round a bend, just missing a donkey laden with pockets of oranges, led by an old man who waved his fist at us, and threw an orange with amazing accuracy.

I tapped the taxi driver on his shoulder.

'We'll get out here,' and he pulled over to the kerb with a flourish.

American dollars were very acceptable, so the fare was paid and he shot off looking for his next passengers.

The chase is on.

I looked around at the bustling scene.

We were in a busy part of town, full of shops and roadside stores, milling with people. The museum entrance was further along the road.

I checked the time with Matilda. It was 1.30pm.

'Where do you think we should wait for the others but still be out of sight?' asked aunt looking around.

'What about that mosque over there? I can see women walking on the parapet. Have you any scarves in your bag? If we cover our heads, I'm sure we'll be allowed in.'

Matilda rummaged in her bag and produced a couple of scarves. We covered our heads and made our way through the teeming crowds, keeping our eyes open for any unwanted attention. We reached the mosque unmolested, and climbed the flight of stairs to the parapet where women were allowed in this male dominated society.

I kept my eyes fixed on the road, waiting for a first glimpse of the land rover. Matilda, fascinated by the gold embossed wall carvings, held a running commentary extolling their virtues.

'When all this is over, Ella, I want to come back here and really explore this place. These carvings are remarkable. They must be hundreds of years old.'

I wasn't listening. The land rover had appeared, earlier than anticipated.

'Quick aunt. We must catch their attention before they turn,' and we ran back down the flight of steps and onto the pavement, and then shot across the road. As luck would have it, the land rover stopped at traffic lights. We scrambled aboard just as the lights changed.

'Don't go to the museum,' I cried, 'Keep driving! It's a trap!'

Jacob grabbed me by the shoulders. 'What happened? Are you all right?'

'I'm fine,' and quickly ran through events leading up to rushing across the road to intercept them.

'So, Ken knew you were going to the museum. Was it just a lucky guess, or what?' remarked Jacob.

'It was strange his accomplice wasn't with them,' said Matilda.

'That's because he was following us, along with that helicopter pilot and Stephanie. We had the devil's own job shaking them off our tail,' replied David.

'Mr Ishmael, the so-called deputy curator, was expecting us to drop in. It's obvious he's up to his neck in the dealings of Swingen Linen. It was handy Mr. Hassan had to make a visit to the interior just at this time.'

I suddenly had a horrible thought.

'I hope the trip was legitimate and not something concocted by Ken and co. It would be terrible if anything happened to Mr. Hassan because of the peacock.'

'Let's not think the worse,' said Cynthia. 'I'm sure Mr Hassan is perfectly fine. The thing is, what do we do next?'

There was a tense silence.

Then Matilda spoke.

'There is only one place left, and that's the Ethiopian embassy.'

'Of course! Well done, aunt. Maybe we should've gone there in the first place. I've got the map. It's bound to have embassies marked on it.'

I unfolded the map and gave my attention to tracking them down. They were all in one area, on the eastern side of town. So, as the museum was on the west, David cut across town.

This was easier said than done. The city was a maze of streets crisscrossing each other with no discernable pattern to them at all.

'I don't think city planning was consulted when Addis Ababa was built. Roads and buildings have just been added on wherever it took somebody's fancy,' grumbled David, as he skilfully negotiated a donkey pulling a cart loaded with sacks of grain.

He narrowly missed a taxi flying out of a side street cutting across the flow of traffic without pausing.

'That's our taxi, I'm sure of it, Ella,' said Matilda fondly, and turned in her seat to watch it disappear.

'Good heavens! Look at that.'

'What aunt?' I asked, swivelling around.

'A taxi just turned in the middle of the road and is now darting in and out of the traffic as though…Oh my, Ella. Look! It's our other attacker!'

And it was, along with Stephanie and the helicopter pilot.

'David! Ken's cohort is after us along with the rest of the gang.'

'I see them, but who's driving the taxi?'

'Would you believe Inspector Stuart done up as a native. But why are they in a taxi? What happened to their cars?'

'We had to scuttle them,' yelled David. 'Hold on!' and he swerved left and right, avoiding cars, pedestrians and animals by inches. It was a magnificent display of driving which Inspector Stuart was unable to emulate. The taxi came to a grinding halt after failing to negotiate a turn and landed up under the stall of a very irate vegetable vendor. We didn't hang around to see the outcome.

Another ten minutes and we were in a quiet part of Addis Ababa. The embassies were housed in grand mansions set back from the tree-lined avenues. Each had a flagpole set in the grounds, flying the flag of the country the embassy represented.

'What does the Ethiopian flag look like?' asked David.

We looked at each other blankly.

Then Cynthia piped up. 'I'll recognize it when I see it.'

'Clever girl,' said David.

Around the next bend, Cynthia pointed to her left.

'There it is.'

AT LAST.

With tyres squealing, we raced up to the guardhouse.

The guard came out running, gun at the ready.

'Sorry about that,' said David, as we skidded to a halt, 'but we're in a hurry to see the ambassador. It literally is a matter of life and death,' he added.

The guard was unimpressed.

'Your passports please,' and held out his left hand, whilst continuing to point his gun at us with the other.

We gave him our passports, and he disappeared into his guardhouse, presumably to phone the embassy with our request.

'Why is he taking so long,' fretted Matilda. 'They'll be on to us soon.'

'I'll crash through those gates if I catch so much as a whiff of that gang,' said David.

The guard sauntered back to the land rover.

'The ambassador wishes to know your business with him.'

'Tell the ambassador the world renowned private investigator and archaeologist Matilda Syndham and her niece Dr Ella Standbridge need to see him urgently on business of national importance. You have seen their passports, and if you don't make it sound good I will hang you out to dry.'

These last words were said as David slowly uncurled his length from the land rover and drew himself up to his full height, towering over the guard who was about five foot six in his socks.

Within minutes, we were driving along a curving driveway leading to the embassy entrance, but with a guard in attendance, rifle at the ready, just in case.

No sooner did the land rover come to a halt; a white uniformed soldier wearing a red fez opened two large, ornately carved wooden doors. He saluted and ushered us into a reception room, richly decorated with gold and scarlet embossed wallpaper. The furniture was just as ornate, consisting of Queen Ann chairs, chaise loungs and glass topped desks and tables, also gold embossed. Tall cut glass vases displayed exotic flowers, their scent intense.

'What a magnificent room,' exclaimed Cynthia.

'You won't catch me sitting on one of those chairs,' remarked David. 'It would collapse under my weight.'

Matilda was spellbound.

She walked around the room, gently touching engravings, smelling the flowers, running her fingers over the richly embroidered upholstery of the furniture.

'You are astonished, no?' said a voice behind us.

We turned and saw a tall bespectacled gentleman standing in the doorway. He was middle aged, a mop of greying hair covering the top of his head like a halo. Under the halo was a pair of brown twinkling eyes peering at us through his spectacles. Perfect gleaming teeth showed in a friendly smile.

He walked into the room, hand outstretched in a welcoming gesture.

'My name is Hussein, Fahmed Hussein. I am the ambassador to my beloved country, Ethiopia. I believe you wanted to see me urgently?'

'Yes, ambassador, very urgently. My name is Matilda Syndham, and this is my niece Ella.'

I shook his hand. What a difference to Ishmael's handshake.

Matilda continued with the introductions.

After handshakes all round, the ambassador suggested going to his office, where we would be more comfortable, and would we like some refreshments? Perhaps some ice tea?

Once settled, we sipped ice tea and nibbled on macaroons, of all things, whilst Matilda told our story.

'You see, ambassador, it all started in my cottage in England, when I found the first body.'

'First body! Is there more than one?' interrupted Ambassador Hussein, looking shocked.

'Oh yes, unfortunately there are. However, let me tell you everything from the beginning, and then you'll understand why we are here.'

It took some telling.

When she'd finished, there was silence.

The ambassador then cleared his throat and said, 'Incredible! I would never have believed such things like this could happen. It sounds like a fiction novel somebody has written.'

He spread his arms wide.

'My friends! You have been through so much, just to see a national treasure restored to its rightful country. The peacock. Where is the peacock now?'

'Right here, ambassador,' and Matilda delved into her carpetbag, lifting out the peacock, still in its sealed box. None of the others had seen it, so everyone moved closer to get a look at the object that had aroused people's passions to such an extent, murder was committed.

Matilda placed the box on the ambassador's desk, broke the seal, lifted the lid and slid her hands inside. Out came the peacock, still wrapped in the soft skin covering. She unfolded the wrapping to reveal the fabulous treasure in all its glory.

There were gasps from Cynthia and David. Jacob murmured something under his breath, and the ambassador... well, he was speechless.

We all feasted our eyes on the shining jewels sparkling like thousands of miniature rainbows. The magnificent diamond, cut in the shape of the Star of David, glowed with a life of its own. The sapphires and emeralds embedded in the tail caused the illusion of feathers moving in the breeze. The peacock was mystically alive.

Jacob was the first to speak.

'Yes, I can understand the spell the peacock would have over people. Matilda, you are right in saying it has to have its home here, otherwise the killing will never end.'

The ambassador asked Matilda if he could hold it.

'But of course, ambassador! It belongs to your country.'

Ambassador Hussein gently cupped his hands around the peacock and lifted it up.

'Mrs Syndham, my government will be forever in your debt. When I think of the danger you have endured to bring the peacock home. How shall we ever repay you?'

'My payment is returning the peacock to where it rightfully belongs, ambassador. Also, I would never have managed it without these wonderful friends, and of course, my niece. All the people of Ethiopia should be allowed to see its beauty.'

'And so they shall, but first we must put it in a safe place until we arrange your not very nice friends to be apprehended.'

The ambassador placed the peacock on the cloth and Matilda wrapped it up and put it back in its box.

'We have a secure safe here at the embassy. You will all come with me and see the peacock locked away so that you yourselves will know it is safe, and will not get into the wrong hands.'

We followed the ambassador along a thickly carpeted passage until we came to a door at the end of the passageway. Ambassador Hussein took a key out of his pocket and unlocked the door.

We entered a room full of filing cabinets, and tucked away behind one of the cabinets was a wall safe. We all looked the other way whilst the ambassador twiddled with the combination, and once the safe was opened, Matilda deposited the peacock into the dark interior.

The door of the safe was closed and locked.

'I shall post a twenty-four hour guard on the door. Your assailants will not be getting their hands on the peacock, I assure you, Mrs. Syndham. Now, it is of the utmost importance we contact the various authorities so these people can be caught.'

'Interpol was our first bet,' said David.

'Yes, Interpol, plus the Ethiopian police. Let us go back to my office where I can get the ball rolling as you say in your delightful country.'

And get the ball rolling is exactly what he did.

The phone lines began buzzing.

Calls were made to Paris, London, Brussels and goodness knows where else. A delegation of Ethiopian police arrived at the embassy to take our statements. Identity pictures were drawn up and wired to all the airports, border posts and seaports in Northern Africa, Europe and the Mediterranean countries. The Swingen Linen offices in London were raided and valuable information obtained on the workings of this international gang of thieves. Warehouses were searched, cargo's confiscated, bank accounts frozen, and the whole network of thieves, couriers, hit men and whoever else was involved, rounded up.

It was quite an operation!

However, it took time, and that time we spent as guests of the Ambassador of Ethiopia in his embassy.

'I could very easily get used to this way of life, aunt,' I said to Matilda, after we'd unpacked our suitcases in one of the guest bedrooms we were sharing.

I looked around the room. Opulence described it. Sheer, unadulterated opulence.

'What do you say, aunt? Could you get used to this type of life?'

No reply.

Matilda was staring ahead, eyes unfocussed.

I touched her shoulder.

'Sorry, Ella. Did you say something?'

'Nothing of importance. Where were you just now? Not in this bedroom, that's for sure.'

She looked at me for a few seconds before answering.

'I was thinking of poor Arthur and what he went through because of the peacock. Still, I'm so relieved that the end of the saga is in sight; although life will seem sadly flat after all the excitement we've been through.'

'Knowing you, aunt, I don't think you'll be resting on your laurels for long and of course we have that other project coming up.'

She laughed, and nodded her head.

I checked the time.

'I said I would meet Jacob in the garden in five minutes. I don't think it would be good to keep the commissioner waiting, now would it,' and I sallied out of the door, outwardly composed, but inwardly feeling like a nervous schoolgirl summoned by the headmistress.

I made my way through the embassy corridors until I came to sliding glass doors leading onto the patio. White painted wooden garden furniture with brightly coloured cushions was arranged around a large umbrella. Jacob was sitting on one of the chairs, nursing a long glass of fresh fruit juice, gazing into the distance.

'Hi Jacob! Are your thoughts at Tevrede?' I asked jokingly.

He stood up and said, 'No, I was thinking of you actually,' and looked at me intently with those black, piercing eyes.

'Let me pour you some juice,' and Jacob filled a glass and handed it to me.

'Well,' I said brightly. 'It looks like we've come to the end of this episode in our lives. Poor Matilda feels quite deflated now that the peacock has been handed over.'

'And you, Ella? How do you feel?'

I thought for a moment.

'A definite sense of satisfaction in finally reaching the end of a long and difficult journey, Plus, I have spoken to my professor who has suggested I return to Africa once everything has settled down. Apparently there are some fascinating ruins in Zimbabwe he thought I might be interested in having a look at. He has already spoken to the officials in the country, paving the way for permission to mount an expedition. I've spoken to Matilda who is keen on the project, and, of course, I am very interested as well. Anyway, enough about me. I suppose you're eager to get back to Tevrede?'

'Yes I am. And guess what? Those ruins your professor is referring to are not that far from the farm.'

Jacob grinned and said, 'the adventure continues. Excellent!'

EPILOGUE

Before we left Ethiopia, the ambassador hosted a banquet, with Matilda as guest of honour.

The peacock was officially handed over to Mr. Hassan, the museum curator. A specially made display cabinet that had all the features of Fort Knox was commissioned for the priceless artefact. It would take an atomic bomb no less to hack into that cabinet.

Mr Ishmael was now languishing in jail, awaiting trial.

David and Cynthia continued on their journey. They took a couple of students along to help them with the driving, although, as Cynthia confided in me, nobody could take the place of the two of us. We continue to stay in touch.

Jacob obviously had to get back to Tevrede.

We shall meet up as soon as the logistics of mounting an expedition to Zimbabwe are completed.

Matilda and I flew back to England to be greeted by the press, which I found rather embarrassing. The archaeological fraternity feted Matilda and gave her an honoury degree by the Fellowship, which tickled her pink!

We obviously had to testify at the trial of Ken and co, Stephanie and Inspector Stuart.

The first three had been picked up trying to get out of Ethiopia using the same caravan route Ackbar used. That was not a good idea. Fisal spotted them haggling with a camel owner; told his grandfather, who got the clan together, and the outcome I'm sure you can imagine.

That reminds me, Fisal is visiting Matilda next June for a summer holiday.

The Swingen Linen gang received hefty prison sentences.

Inspector Stuart was caught boarding a fishing vessel, of all things, at Mombasa. He admitted murdering Jacob's father because of the scarf but was unable to find it.

Jacob's father, it was thought, had contacted Frederick Short and Philip Westbury a couple of months before his death, or they could have contacted him first. Whichever way, contact had been made.

However, Jacob and his mother had been totally unaware of this.

Uncle and nephew had one scarf; Jacob's father had another, and Philip had found the third in Matilda's cottage, but was murdered by Ken and co before he could do anything with it. Matilda walked into the cottage just after the murder had happened and in their haste to skedaddle left Matilda's scarf behind.

Inspector Stuart was the mastermind.

He had direct access to all the security arrangements made for transportation and storage of art treasures throughout the world. Frederick Short had been recruited by Stephanie Stone as a go-between for the various treasures stolen, or were requested to be stolen by unscrupulous collectors.

However, he tried to double cross the inspector when he and Philip between them decided to hunt for the peacock themselves after finding out the silk scarves were the main key to hunting down the treasure.

Mr Short had purloined one scarf from the Swingen Linen offices. He knew Matilda had been given one by mistake, and, of course, Jacob's father had one. Hence, Philip making my acquaintance, and if the inspector hadn't ordered their demise when he found out about the double cross, they would have gone to Tevrede to look for the other scarf, and would probably have found the peacock, and it would have been lost to the world forever.

Matilda and I were the inspector's worst nightmare.

Apparently, he ranted and raved about us as he was led away to the cells. We had stopped him earning several million pounds in commission from the collector who wanted to scoop the peacock. No wonder he called me a flaming nuisance!

So, we come to the end of the story of the peacock.

Oh, not quite.

Are you still wondering about the grandfather clock showing eight instead of twelve?

No mystery there actually.

Blame it on a mouse nest!

About the Author

I have lived in different parts of Africa for many years. This is where the idea for the book came from.

Printed in the United States
By Bookmasters